# Bradley H. Sinor
# PULP WRITER

Airship 27 Productions

TM

Bradley H. Sinor Pulp Writer
All stories ©2022 Bradley H. Sinor

Published by Airship 27 Productions
www.airship27.com
www.airship27hangar.com

Interior Illustrations © 2022 Warren Montgomery
Cover illustraion © 2022 Rob Davis

Editor: Ron Fortier
Associate Editor: Rob Davis
Marketing and Promotions Manager: Michael Vance
Production and design by Rob Davis

ISBN: 978-1-953589-42-2

Printed in the United States of America

10 9 8 7 6 5 4 3 2 1

## Bradley H. Sinor
# PULP WRITER

# Contents

# SILVER EYES

The house had definitely seen better days, that much was obvious the first time anyone laid eyes on the place.

When Reese climbed out of the back of the van he couldn't have cared less. Just being here was something that he had been dreaming about every night for the six months he had spent in the Hancock County jail.

As Reese came across the yard he found himself smiling when he spotted the tiny brass Buddha made of tarnished and dented base metal, sitting on the small altar of bricks and boards it had occupied for years. No one knew who put it there; it was just one of those things that had always been near the house.

The snow had melted for an inch or so around the statue, leaving it surrounded by wet wood. Very carefully, with the utmost respect, Reese reached down and touched it, with his ungloved hand, letting his body heat melt the few remaining flecks of snow away.

A long steep metal stairway led to the second floor of the house. Several decades ago, he suspected, there had been an elaborately covered landing marking the entrance to what was now his apartment. That however was long done, replaced by a rusting metal stairway.

It took several attempts before he could pull the spare door key free from the crack in the wood that was its hiding place. As he stood there for a moment before fitting it into the lock, Reese noticed his reflection in the window. His hair was shorter than he preferred; that had been part of the dress code at the jail. All inmates had to have short hair. Clean-shaven and shorthaired was the way the county authorities wanted their charges to return to the "real world". And that was how Reese had returned home.

That they hadn't required a buzz cut was fine. That would have brought back too many memories of the Marines, ones that he preferred not to deal with. A razor hadn't touched his face since his release and wouldn't until his goatee had regrown.

On the wall in the kitchen was a list of repairs to the house that he and Dale, who owned the place, had compiled nearly a year ago. That nothing had been marked off didn't surprise Reese in the least. Dale was a good guy, but he did tend to get distracted by other projects before the first ones he started were completed.

The only source of heat for the apartment came from the kitchen stove and a few electric floor heaters, and that was normally more than enough.

As decrepit as the house was, Reese felt like he could sense an echo of the people who had lived in it over the years. At a Rainbow Gathering in an Oregon national park, an Irish girl had told him he had the sight and was in touch with a lot of places where the others, the people who had gone before, still walked.

Reese had never claimed that he really understood what she met, but her words felt right. Of course, so had she when they had gone back to her tent in the wee hours of the morning.

Pushing the door to the bedroom open, he found it illuminated by a dozen candles, each of a different size. On a mattress, a woman dressed in a semitransparent black gown that matched her short died black curls sat on a mattress that had been pushed up against the wall.

"Took you long enough to get here," she said. In the two years since they had met on the beach where they had both been sleeping near Cabo San Lucas, there had not been a day when Adrianna had been far from his thoughts. Her visits and the knowledge that she would be waiting for him had helped him get through some of the very long nights in the Hancock County jail.

"Adrianna," he whispered.

"Glad you remembered my name," she said, smiling, patting a space next to her on the mattress. "Now come here and show me how much you missed me."

"So, did you get a lot written since the last time I was down here?" Reese had drifted into writing poetry after he got out of the Marines. A few of them had seen print in alternative newspapers and small press magazines.

"Yeah, sort of. They wouldn't let me have any pens, just pencils, and loose pages. Some sort of idea that I might use an ink pen to dig an escape tunnel or something like that," he said.

"Later you can read me some of them, but only if you read me the comic strips." Adrianna didn't like to read the newspaper but she adored the daily comic strips.

Reese chuckled as she reached across him to where she had left her purse, buried in the folds of her dress. She extracted a package of chewing gum and pulled two pieces out. According to her, it was her only bad habit. She crumpled the wrappers and dropped them in her purse as she popped them into her mouth.

"I'm so glad you're back," she sighed, laying her head on his chest. Reese moved his arm up to allow her to snuggle closer. Before he slipped off to sleep the last thing he clearly remembered was the feeling of the gentle movement of her breathing.

*Silver eyes*

*In the distance, at the far end of the park, Reese could see some kids playing. It was some sort of complicated scenario involving swings and cardboard boxes; the sort of thing that makes perfect sense to anyone ten years old or younger and is utterly incomprehensible to anyone older.*

He stood and watched them for a few minutes, not understanding what he saw, just enjoying the scene. Turning away and heading away from the playground, he realized that he had no clear memory of how he had gotten there, or even where there was.

Reese was being watched, he knew that, had known it from the first moment he had realized he was in the park. He couldn't say by whom, any more than he could say how he knew it was by someone with Silver Eyes.

Reese noticed the difference as soon as he walked in the door of The Sundown Club; part coffee house, part bar, part performance space, it served as a gathering place for people who were not anywhere near part of the mainstream. There were new couches, fresh paint, and tables that did not look like they had been scrounged from the reject pile at a Burger King. The old look had character, but the new one did, too. It would take some getting used to.

The main room that took up most of the bottom floor had a good feel to it, not just from the collection of people who filled it: everything from Goths like Adrianna to bikers to hippies like Reese. At one end of the room was a performance space large enough for a band or single performer. Right now, a single microphone and a stool stood in the center, silently waiting for someone to claim the space.

"I'll get us something," she said, heading for the bar at the other end of the room.

Reese watched the gentle sway of her hips as she walked away, the beaded velvet black skirt moving gently. They made an unusual couple —Adrianna in her Goth black and velvet, him in jeans, boots, and an old Marine BDU jacket. The Hippie and The Goth, it sounded like something out of a bad fifties movie or a country and western song.

In the middle of all the chatter around him, Reese froze when one sound cut through the din. The sharp snap of an old-fashioned metal lighter being opened and closed three times quickly in succession.

*Karl?*

He looked, not knowing what to expect, almost afraid that he would see a small dark-haired figure with an infectious smile and ever-present Zippo lighter, not certain what he would do, considering that Karl Edgar was dead and had been for five years.

"Hey, man, it's about ruddy time you showed your ass around here. What took you so long?" Reese looked over at a small man, barely five feet tall, perching against the side of the couch and looking at him. Chancy was one of his oldest friends. They had grown up together; he had even driven Reese to the bus the day he had left for boot camp.

"Hey, had my hands full," said Reese. "You know how popular I am. They just didn't want to let me go. I don't think they wanted to have to admit that they couldn't do without me."

"That's the price of fame." Chancy's expression grew serious and his voice dropped almost to a whisper. "You did a good thing, man, a good thing. Devon could never have taken the time inside. The only way he would have come out would have been feet first."

"What can I say, little brother, I'm just a force for good in my time." It wasn't as if he had felt he had any choice at the time. Devon Carmichael had been stupid; there was no doubt about that. He had pulled over to the side of the road so he could flip off a pair of police officers who were writing tickets for several bikers.

Reese had managed to get Devon out of the driver's seat and taken his place before the cop descended on them. The police finding half a bag of grass and some assorted pills in the spare tire didn't surprise Reese. But even knowing that, he knew he would have done the same thing. That's what you did for a friend if they needed the help.

"So when are you going to come back?"

Reese looked up with a start to see Adrianna standing where Chancy had been, a gentle smile on her face; his old friend had wandered off. She held a couple of bottles of beer and a paper plate filled with French fries and a big glob of ketchup.

"Come back? I just got back, which I sort of think you kind of noticed. Don't you have to leave to be able to come back to someplace?" he asked.

"Yes, I did notice that," she said settling down on one of the couches. "It was that look on your face. I've seen it before. You were a long way away from here. Care to share your itinerary."

"Not right now," he said, not even sure exactly what he would say to her if he had been inclined to talk.

"When you're ready," Adriana said.

As he took a swallow of beer, washing down a handful of fries, Reese heard the sound of a Zippo lighter being flipped open three times, in quick succession, again.

"I'll be back," Reese muttered, gesturing toward the restrooms. Adrianna nodded; she was deep into a conversation with a woman in a dress with tarot designs on it.

The back steps of the club led to an alley that ran the length of the block. There was no sign that anyone had been there; the ruts and footprints that marred the snow were not fresh. Out of the corner of his eye he caught sight of someone coming toward him; a blonde-haired woman in a leather jacket that hung to her ankles.

"Long time no see, Spooky," he said.

"That's Mistress Stephanie to you," the woman replied, with just a touch of sarcasm in her voice.

"Yeah, right," he said.

He had known Stephanie Dixon since junior high school. For a time the two had dated, two outsiders finding solace in each other. But they had learned they were better friends than lovers, especially when Stephanie had come to realize that her attraction was to women. Yet the friendship had remained. It had been Reese who dubbed her Spooky.

"Damn, it's good to see you, Reese." Spooky smiled a come-hither smile as she pulled him into a hug. "I heard you were back, figured if I could find you anyplace, it would be at the Sundown."

"That hurts," he said as he pulled back slightly, the sharp edges of the zippers, the studs and rings on her clothes cutting into him.

He ran his eyes up and down her leather-clad figure. "How can you breathe in that getup? It looks so tight that you couldn't get a stick of chewing gum between your skin and the clothes. I certainly wouldn't advise you to do any heavy breathing."

"Heavy breathing, sir?" she said, slipping into a faux southern accent. "When Mistress Stephanie goes to work it's my clients who do the heavy breathing, even if I have to whip it out of them."

That made sense. Spooky was a dominatrix. She had discovered where her "talents" lay at an early age. Once she had realized that there was good money to be made, she quickly developed a thriving private practice, with a client list that included many movers and shakers in local political and social circles.

Not a year ago she had opened her own place, just down the street from the Sundown, that catered to those with a taste for the sort of entertainment she was used to providing, called, appropriately, "Spooky's."

Reese had, on occasion, worked security at Spooky's. He'd seen a lot of unusual things in his travels, but Reese had to admit that a few of the things that had gone on inside Spooky's had surprised even him.

"I'll bet when you fly you really have fun going through the metal detectors at the airport."

"Hey, when I fly I am Ms Prim and Proper, in a tailored Donna Karin power suit that would make The Donald willing to hire me. Hell, I even take off the clit ring."

"I bet that Lynda really loves that," he said

Even in the dark, Reese could see something was wrong. Spooky didn't say anything, but she shifted just a bit, let out a deep breath, and stared down at the ground. Lynda and Spooky had met several years ago and it had been like they had always known each other.

"What happened?"

"The wrong place at the wrong time, four months ago. She had stopped to get some Chinese food for dinner. A Meth head was trying to rob the place. He shot her five times. She didn't have a chance."

The tears that rolled down Spooky's face were out of place with her outfit. Reese put his arm around her and pulled Stephanie close, hoping to wipe the pain away for a moment or two with the knowledge that she was safe and loved. His hand brushed against the silver slave bracelet on her left arm; it wasn't necessary to look, he knew that Lynda's name was on it.

"I'd do anything if I could have her back," said Stephanie.

"Incoming!"

Reese was already in the process of throwing himself into a doorway when he heard Cpl. Karl Edgar's warning. Even an hour after dawn the air was heavy with heat and dirt.

There were a couple of swift explosions on the street. Reese heard Edgar on the radio, reporting in to battalion command. Their job this morning had been to move along the western end of the town, just a few blocks along a side street, then the two of them were to link back up with the rest of the patrol.

"See anything?" yelled Reese. The civilians had dived for cover, for a moment leaving the street with an abandoned movie set feel.

"Nothing," answered Karl. In the nearly a year that the Marines had been on this "peacekeeping" assignment, unexpected attacks like this had become daily occurrences.

"Another fun day in the Middle East," he said. "What the hell?" Reese turned toward his friend. The other Marine was pointing into an alley. Two figures were on the ground, one crouching over the other, a radiance moving from one into the other that cycled from blue through purple and back again.

Karl headed toward them, his M16 spitting fire. One of them, who looked like a preteenager dressed in rags, stood up, leaving the other one to collapse in a heap like a marionette with its strings cut. For only a heartbeat the child's figure was replaced by a seething mass of slime-colored tentacles and teeth and eyes, hundreds of eyes. The radiance shot forward from it and enveloped Karl, shattering him into blood-soaked pieces.

Reese had to pull back; the light was so bright that it was painful. The world dropped away from Reese, and the last thing he remembered was the boy's silver eyes.

Reese came fully awake; his face stinging like someone had slapped him, but the room was empty. Adrianna had left for her graveyard shift job at the cell phone call center on the south side of town. Not that she really liked the job. She was known to refer to it as the Hellhole or the ninth circle of Hell. But it was also a regular paycheck; she had come to recognize the necessity of that.

The distinct sound of the door closing and footsteps on the stairway caught Reese's full attention. When he looked out of the window there was no one in sight, but he thought he caught a glimpse of a figure disappearing into an alley.

Only the light from the twenty-four-hour convenience store across the alley broke the darkness. There were no cars in the parking lot and even the wind had died away. When Reese walked through the door the clerk nodded, said his required greeting, and then went back to the paperwork that was spread out on the table behind the counter.

After buying a can of soda, Reese stood at the door, staring outside, not certain what to do now. His gut told him that the whole thing was real, but it had assumed an almost surreal quality to him.

Looking out the door, he caught sight of something lying in the snow against the wall. Stepping out, he reached down and picked it up, shaking the snow off. It was a silver slave bracelet, connected by a chain to a ring, identical to the one Spooky wore, the name Stephanie engraved across the back.

"Excuse me," said the clerk, holding a phone in his hand.

"Yeah?"

"Your name wouldn't happen to be Reese, would it?"

"That's me."

"It's for you." He held up the receiver. It was on a cord so Reese had to come back to the counter.

"This is Reese."

"You might want to stop by the club," said Lynda. "Oh, and bring back my bracelet."

Reese didn't have a valid driver's license, though it had been high on his list of acquisitions, lack of legal documentation was never something that had bothered him. In the shed just behind the house was a motorcycle, a thirty-year-old Harley Davidson.

Rolling it down the inclined driveway, Reese waited until he was a half block from the house before trying to start it. Two attempts were all that he needed; hotwiring had been one of the skills he had acquired before he was in high school.

Ten minute's ride and he was braking to a stop behind the club. There were times when the windows danced with light until dawn. This was not one of them. Every window was dark and the whole structure had an abandoned feel to it. Using a pry bar, he let himself in the delivery door.

Reese could hear sounds coming from the main part of the club. It took a moment to realize that it was singing. Saying that whoever was doing the singing did not have the best voice in the world would not have been stretching the truth, especially when he realized the song was "Tip Toe through the Tulips". Something along the lines of an Ennio Morricone spaghetti western soundtrack would have more fit the moment.

Twin spotlights flooded down to form an oasis of light on the stage. Around it were tables, each with a throne-like chair and a wooden frame next to it with straps at each corner and a selection of whips laid along the bottom.

One of the frames was on the stage, sitting in the circle of light, bent backward until it was almost horizontal. Spooky was strapped into it; her pale white skin, crisscrossed by multiple red welts, seemed to glow in the bright clear unfiltered light coming from above. A dozen candles had been placed around Spooky's tits, face, and stomach. Thin pillars of black smoke arose from the ones where the flames had been put out.

The singing continued, from someone who stood just outside the pool of light. On a high note, the stinging end of a leather whip shot out, missing the candle and cutting its mark into the soft flesh of Spooky's neck. Spooky let out a low moan, her eyes clamped shut as tears rolled down her cheeks.

Reese came around the frame, grabbed the assailant, and pulled them close enough to see. It was a woman wearing nothing but cut-off jeans and a black merry widow corset.

Lynda.

"Hey, big man," laughed Lynda as she pulled herself loose from his grip and walked over to Spooky. With two fingers she pinched one of the candles out, then ran her hand along Spooky's arm like it was a delicate flower. "Come to rescue the poor innocent maiden?"

Reese felt like he was in a dream, a completely topsy-turvy world where the dead were walking and the livings were puppets on strings.

That was when another voice was heard, coming from one of the big chairs near the stage. "Oh come on, are you just going to stand there with your jaw hanging open,

Reese? That is so pussy-whipped pathetic. I really expected more from you." The speaker was a preteen boy, dressed in skater's regalia - drooping pants, basketball shirt, and do-rag.

Reese felt his stomach tightening, it was the face of the same preteen boy he had seen killing Karl. For just that moment he saw the pulsating thing of tentacles and silver eyes, and then it became the boy again, the silver eyes glowing as they had in his dreams all these years.

"What the hell are you?" asked Reese.

"Give me a break," the boy said. "I told you I expected more out of you. You've known I would be coming after you for a long time."

"If it's me you want, why involve Spooky?" demanded Reese.

"Good question. The answer is, why not? I made her an offer and she accepted it, even on my terms. Hey, when you've got the connections I do, why not use them."

Reese remembered her words as they had stood in the alley. *"I'd do anything if I could have her back,"*

"Plus, it got you here to let me do some housekeeping; you know, clean up some loose ends from a few years ago. I don't really like leaving people around who have seen me, bad public relations and all that."

Lynda moved up beside Reese. She ran her hand across his chest. Instinctively he reached out and pushed her away, hard enough to send her sprawling onto the floor.

"So what are you going to do, me bucko? Maybe beat the hell out of Lynda, like the real man that you are. Or why don't you cut to the chase, the two of us go mano a mano."

Reese smiled. It was a gesture without emotion. He felt himself slipping back into that place inside him where the warrior, the killer lived, the place he had abandoned when he had left the Marines. The thing in front of him, he would not let himself think of it as human despite the face it wore, began to laugh.

"Reese." It was Spooky, her voice a hoarse whisper.

"Aw, isn't that just so sweet? Actually, it's kind of a turn-on, as well. Hey, I got an idea, why don't you just fuck her. I think she and you both would enjoy it. Lynda and I can watch!"

"Reese." He leaned down close, never once taking his eyes off the figure on the other side of the frame. Spooky's words came slowly, each breath a labored struggle.

"You're sure?" he asked a moment later.

She nodded. Reese leaned forward and kissed her, drawing her lips tightly to him. When they separated he whispered, "So long, Stephanie."

Turning and walking away was the hardest thing that Reese had ever done; each step was a struggle. Every instinct in him wanted to tear into the thing, to rip it into tiny bloody pieces and feel the life ebb out of its flesh, though on another level he knew that he would face the same fate Karl had if he attacked it.

Behind him, he could hear the boy screaming challenge after challenge at him, impugning his ancestry and suggesting an interest in certain barnyard animals. As he headed down the hallway he could hear the snap of the whip, and "Tip Toe through the Tulips."

"You look like hell."

Three quick snaps of a Zippo lighter followed that remark. Reese smiled at the sound.

"For a guy who has been dead and buried for five years, you are the last person to be talking about someone else's appearance," laughed Reese. After he had returned the cycle to its parking place, Reese had dropped down at the bottom of the stairway leading to his apartment and just sat there, not able to motivate himself to walk upstairs.

Karl Edgar, late of the United States Marine Corps, stood near the stairway. He was dressed in a BDU jacket and jeans. Karl seemed unaffected by the passing of years and that minor inconvenience called death.

"I'm looking damn good right now," laughed Karl.

"So, are you really here?" asked Reese. "Aren't you supposed to have moved on to another plane of existence?"

"Damned if I know. I just know I'm where I need to be right now. You did good tonight, Reese."

"I did good? I left Spooky! You do know what she told me?

"Yeah, I know," said Karl.

When he heard Spooky's words, "This is what I want." He had hoped it was one of that "thing's" tricks, but he had known in his gut that it wasn't. He had known that there was nothing he could do. That was what hurt, not being able to do something; it felt like he had failed Stephanie.

Karl dropped a newspaper onto Reese's lap. It was folded open to a story about a fire that had destroyed the "controversial" club called Spooky's. The body of the owner had been found inside; the matter was still under investigation. This didn't hit him as hard as he would have expected.

Spooky had said that she felt incomplete without Lynda. At least now they were together.

"Yeah, I know what she said," Karl told him. "But by not doing anything, that was the best way, the only way to fight that _thing_. It couldn't attack you; it could only react. If you didn't throw a punch it was helpless, frustrated, and angry, but helpless nonetheless. You would have been toast just like me if you had gone after it."

"What was it anyway?"

"Don't ask me. Being dead doesn't give you access to all knowledge. Call it a demon, call it a manifestation of the Id and the Ego, call it Spooky's madness crossing your own insanity, I just know that you fought it the only way it can be fought."

"I just felt like I should have done something else, anything."

"Live with it," said Karl.

"I don't suppose I have much choice."

"Choice about what?" Reese looked up with a start. His old friend, or the waking dream he had been having of him, was nowhere to be seen. Adrianna stood in his place on the far side of the stairway looking at him.

"Don't worry about it. Did you have a good night at work?"

"It blew, but you know that. I figured I would find you sound asleep, sprawled over your side of the bed, and mine as well." She laughed, leaning over to kiss him on the cheek.

"I woke up and decided to take a walk." He looked over at the Buddha, then reached over and touched it gently on the head. "Figured I would wear myself out that way and actually get some sleep."

"Forget that idea. I have plans for you, sir, plans that will get you tired enough to sleep," she said, slipping her arm through his and pulling him to his feet.

"Plans?"

"Yes, you're going to bed with me," she said as they started up the stairway. "And do you know what you are going to do first?"

"What?"

She held up the newspaper. "Read me the comic strips."

## The End

# AT BEST AN ECHO

"**E**lena," muttered Abraham Van Helsing as he looked down at the silver-framed photograph in his hand. The flickering light from the gas flame on the wall covered the glass with a yellow glare. It wasn't necessary to see the picture; he knew each and every inch of it.

It had been taken six months after Elena and he had been married in 1880. The two of them were stiff and unmoving, waiting as the photographer got everything ready to expose the plate. He had his hand resting on her shoulder as she perched on a small stool, a parasol across her knees. But there was a gleam in Elena's eyes, hinting that she was a moment away from saying something either profound or amazingly funny. That was the woman he loved.

He flexed the fingers of his hands, still remembering the feel of her hand in his, and his fingers wrapped tightly around a sharp obsidian knife. He wiped away a single tear as he stared at the picture.

"Abraham, have you gone deaf?"

Van Helsing looked up with a start. On some level, he had heard his name being spoken, one of any number of sounds that echoed up and down the halls of the University

Of Amsterdam's Medical School.

He blinked twice and realized that a familiar figure had invaded his office. The tall, imposing figure of Dr. Joseph Bell, a black medical bag in his hand, stood there smiling. Bell was sixty-three years old, but with the amount of energy he seemed to radiate, and despite the shock of white hair, the man could easily have passed for twenty years younger.

"Joseph! It's good to see you," Van Helsing advanced toward his friend. Bell's grip was still strong.

The two had known each other for more than two decades since they had investigated a matter involving a plague and an alleged curse. Bell was the first one to scoff and proclaim the supernatural events that Van Helsing had investigated to be nothing but folkloric poppycock and mummery. That had not stopped the two of them from becoming friends.

"What are you doing here at this time of the year? I believe that the semester is not yet over," said Van Helsing, filling two glasses with sherry and passing one to his friend. "I would have expected you to be terrorizing medical students to the point that they would prefer those bleak Scottish winters to missing one of your lectures."

"Indeed, these are the final weeks of winter term. Some of my colleagues seemed to think I have been working too hard, so I asked Arthur Doyle to fill in for a while and decided to come here for a visit," said Bell.

"So, Abraham, I see the food is still excellent at the Medlenbrough," Bell continued.

"Up to your usual tricks, Joseph?" Van Helsing made no effort to conceal his actions as he glanced down at his sleeves and pants legs looking for any telltale sign that might have given Bell any clues to his eating habits.

"I would hardly call my minor observations tricks," Bell told him. "It is just the skill of a good diagnostician, a skill that every doctor should have."

"I know what you look for and how you are able to diagnose these things about people, but it still amazes me," chuckled Van Helsing.

"In this case, it was just two things: in the pocket of your overcoat, I noticed the Daily Journal. The Medlenbrough always stocks the latest papers for its morning patrons. Since the date on the paper is today's, and the delivery label with the name of the hotel is clearly visible, I was able to make my conclusion."

"And the second thing?" said Van Helsing.

"Your appointment book is open on your desk. I noticed that you had written that you could be reached at the hotel between 8:00 and 10:00 this morning," said Bell.

"As always, obvious and elementary," Van Helsing said. He saw the wince on Bell's face at the context of the last word. "Once again I see the reason that young Doyle modeled that detective of his on you."

"Humph," said Bell. "The less said about that, the better, I should think."

Bell picked up the medical bag he had carried in and set it in front of Van Helsing. From inside it, he brought out a small leather folio. "I want you to know that I have violated several British laws in obtaining this for you."

Van Helsing picked it up and unfastened the leather ties that held it closed. Inside were a dozen parchment pages. The material felt odd, different, and not just from age. The only other time he had felt anything similar had been in one of the most guarded rooms in the British Museum. He had gone there to consult copies of the Al Azief, the so-called Necronomicon, and other volumes that it was better the British public did not know about.

"All that remains of the Kollier-Croft Codex," he murmured.

"I thought you might recognize it; apparently a few pages were salvaged," said Bell.

"Indeed. I've been trying to get a look at this for five years since I first learned of its existence. Baron Carlson refused to even admit that he had it," said Van Helsing.

"Oh, he had it, all right. Let us say that saving the life of the Baron's grandson gave me a bit more leverage than you had. I made a weekend visit to his country home, and this came away with me. I just borrowed it, of course," said Bell.

Exactly how Bell had managed that bit of prestidigitation, Van Helsing could only speculate. He had heard rumors of how well it, and the rest of the Baron's occult library, was hidden. Yet it didn't surprise him that his friend had been able to acquire the codex pages.

"If you were willing to take that risk, Joseph, have you come to believe that the secrets in these pages will enable me to help Elena?" said Van Helsing.

"I believe that you believe they will, old friend. If having this helps you, it was worth the risk," said Bell. "I only wish the way out of that padded room was in them."

Van Helsing had spread the pages out on his desk, pushing everything else off to the side. Written in Greek and Latin, the pages appeared to be part of a traveler's narrative; illustrated with some highly detailed renderings of animals and plants. The writing was crabbed in places, running letters together as if the writer had been rushed and uncertain if he would be able to finish.

As he read line after line, Van Helsing found himself thinking of a Latin tutor he'd had as a boy of nine. The Reverend James Murray had been convinced that his young charge would never master the tongue of Rome.

After several minutes the text began to change, letters blurring and reforming, the illustrations changing as well into things that no naturalist of any age had described. No longer was he looking at a travel narrative, but descriptions of horrific ancient ceremonies spells that invoked powers and beings from the darkest places of the universe.

Van Helsing laid his finger a quarter of the way down one page, tracing a circular symbol. The pen work was painfully fine and detailed, leaving the impression of one drawing carefully lain on another, layer upon layer.

Looking at it, he had the feeling of standing at the bottom of a huge mural and being able to see only a tiny bit of it. The desire to see the rest, to know its secrets, was like a tidal wave rolling over him, obliterating his awareness of everything else.

"*Abraham, no!*" The voice was female, distant but clear and commanding.

Van Helsing jerked backward, his vision filled with the familiar sights of his university office. He had to struggle to draw a breath, grabbing onto the edge of the desk to steady himself.

Bell sprinted across the room, grabbing his friend by the arm, as Van Helsing's legs went out from underneath him. The Scotsman managed to guide the other man into the chair.

"Easy there, Abraham," Bell said as he loosened Van Helsing's tie and began to check his pulse.

"I'm all right."

"That's a matter of opinion," said Bell. "You're as pale as a ghost. Your heart is hammering like you had just run a marathon. I turn my back for only a minute, then it's like a hurricane hit this room, everything goes flying, and you drop like a stringless marionette."

"Did I do this?" He gestured at the scattered items on the floor.

"I'm reasonably certain that you did since we are alone in here," Bell said. "That is, unless you have a resident ghost."

"That would be a simple explanation."

"Simple explanations are sometimes the best. But let's leave all explanations till later. Perhaps we should call a halt to this matter, at least for the moment," suggested Bell. "I think a bite of supper might be good for you. May I suggest we adjourn to the Medlenbrough?"

"That might help," agreed Van Helsing.

Since the weather was terrible, it had been raining for two days straight; the dining room at The Medlenbrough was nearly empty. Not that they would have been denied a choice of tables under other circumstances, but the maître d' knew Van Helsing well, so there was little doubt that they would get a good table.

"So, you just walked off and left your students," said Van Helsing as he bit into the last piece of his filet.

"Indeed I did. Call it their holiday from me. Since everyone had been nagging at me to take some time off, I decided to do it, just not when they thought I would. Another matter brought me here." Bell produced an envelope from inside his jacket and passed it over to Van Helsing. "That young Dr. Simmons that you wrote me about seems perfectly suited to fill the position in the medical school. I thought I would bring his acceptance letter myself, but I think you should have the pleasure of actually giving it to him."

"You have made a wise choice. Mark will be an asset to your staff, although it will be quite a transition from the University of Amsterdam to watching the misty dawns over Edinburgh Castle."

"I should say so," said Bell. "Just be sure you caution him to be ready for our Scottish winters. They are a bit more brisk than you have been experiencing here."

Van Helsing inclined his head for a moment as he noticed a small man dressed in a dark, slightly rumpled, suit approaching their table.

"Good evening, Inspector," he said.

"Good evening, Herr Professor. I am sorry to disturb your dinner. They told me at the University that you were dining here."

"Don't trouble yourself, Inspector Hollaman. Allow me to present my friend and colleague, Dr. Joseph Bell of the University of Edinburgh. Joseph, this is James Augustus Hollaman, one of the bright lights of the Amsterdam police department."

"A pleasure, Inspector," said Bell.

"The pleasure is mine, Herr Doctor. I hope you will forgive the intrusion. I need to discuss a matter of great importance with Prof. Dr. Van Helsing."

"Anything you can say to me you can say to Dr. Bell; he is utterly trustworthy," said Van Helsing.

"Sir, you must come with me. There has been an incident at the asylum that resulted in a death," said the policeman.

"At the asylum?" Van Helsing felt the color draining out of his face.

"Yes. Someone tried to murder your wife."

Once he was certain that his wife was safe, Van Helsing requested to be allowed to see her attacker. The body had been removed deep into the basement, below the most secure cells, into the asylum's morgue. Lit with several gas lamps, it was filled with shadows and silence. There was a smell of disinfectant hanging in the air above the stone and the mortar, mixed with a cold that seemed to leach what little warmth the three men had brought into the room with them.

What lay on the table looked human, at first glance. Van Helsing lifted one of its hands and could see the webbing between the fingers, which also seemed to have an extra joint. Pulling back the eyelids, the orbs that

"Someone tried to murder your wife."

looked out were solid black with almost no sign of white except at the very edges.

"An extraordinary example of deformity," said Bell. "It was only a matter of luck that the attendants saw him going into your wife's room. I just wish they hadn't killed him. Though from what they said, it was the only way to keep him from killing Elena."

"Thankfully, there will be no reports in the newspapers regarding this incident," said Hollaman. "I have already had a word with some of our friends in the fourth estate. I will leave you doctors to examine the body. He carried papers identifying him as one Eban Marsh, an American sailor from Massachusetts. I want to check in with the officers I have assigned to watch the asylum for the rest of the night."

On a table near the body was the attacker's weapon, a curved dagger. The blade was some six inches long, but the curve and its shiny surface gave it a feeling of being longer. The handle was covered in intricate designs, portraying several strange creatures, tentacles wrapped around symbols carved into the wood.

"This is a priceless bit of work," said Bell. "The skill that went into it is amazing. From the color of the wood, I would venture to suggest that it is old, perhaps several generations."

"I concur," Van Helsing said. "It would have been passed down from one generation to the next. All dedicated to the same thing."

"Such as?" asked Bell.

Van Helsing pointed at several places on the handle, showing how the design went from the wood onto the metal itself. "These symbols are pictographs, used by some obscure South Seas tribes. Loosely translated, it seems to describe this weapon as being the sting from beyond the edge and the dark of Nyarlathotep and Yog Sog Oth."

"Part of the Cthulhu mythological cycle, as I recall," Bell said.

"A bit more than myth, I would say," observed Van Helsing.

Bell seemed to be ignoring him, intent on examining the appendages of the corpse, moving the joints in most unusual ways. "This "person" is either one of the most deformed beings in existence, or there has been a tremendous amount of inbreeding."

"Inbreeding, yes, with a good bit of cross-species breeding, as well," said Van Helsing. "Let us hope that our friend's "cousins" do not come calling or attempt to reclaim his body."

Bell motioned at the dagger. "Certainly not if they are that well-armed."

"Joseph, if you would continue your examination of the body, I would appreciate it."

"I was wondering when you would go to see *her*." It was a statement rather than a question; one that Van Helsing knew needed no answer.

Standing in front of the door to Elena's room, Van Helsing was afraid. He knew what he wanted to find on the other side of the door, but he knew what he would find, and they were two different things.

The door, a heavy metal thing, swung silently open. The windows were closed, sealed shut with wire mesh and bars. There were other locks on the room, tiny, carefully inscribed symbols, tiny bits of salt, incense, and oil, discreetly spread into the four corners, protections against things that only a few, outside of those who were strangers to sanity, knew existed.

From out in the hallway, he could hear the sound of footsteps and distant screaming cries of other patients, the same sounds that Elena had heard every day and night for the past dozen years.

Elena was lying completely still in her bed, covered partially by a blanket. Her face was awash in the shadows and bits of light that leaked in from the hallway, relaxed and, for a moment, at peace, even with lines of pain in her face and ragged streaks of gray marking her hair.

Her eyes were open, staring straight at the ceiling, marked only by the slow blinking of the lids. Van Helsing looked at her for a long time as he stood next to the bed, then leaned forward until his face was only inches from hers.

"Elena," he said softly and began to sing softly to her. The tune was a Welch folk song they had heard in those long-gone first days after they had met. When Elena heard it she proclaimed it wonderful and insisted on learning the music and words.

For several minutes there was only Van Helsing's voice, but then he began to hear hers; echoing each note and tone that came from him. It was a tiny sad sound that came from Elena's throat. She had done this before, many times, and then it would be gone, as quickly as it had begun. Van Helsing allowed himself the slim hope that this would be the moment he had prayed for. That this was the fanning of the flame, that it would light her way out of the prison of insanity that he had locked her in.

"The walkers slide with the penguins quietly," she said in a little girl's voice.

"Elena," he said, his heart breaking as he heard the words.

"Abraham," Elena said in a clear and precise voice." I wanted to go for a walk like we did that first day, but the hurling monkeys are blocking our way."

She began to hum, and then the sound faded away. Without warning Elena Van Helsing sat straight up in her bed, as stiff as a board, shooting up so quickly that she almost collided with her husband. She stayed like that for a moment, then slid back onto her bed, lying as silently as the darkness around her.

Three candles and a piece of chalk were all that Van Helsing needed after he had returned to the asylum with the leather folio. It had taken him nearly an hour to draw the complicated design, filling up much of the room as it wrapped around his wife's bed.

None of the staff had come into the room except for a single orderly who said nothing, just stood in the doorway looking at the scene in front of him, and left. Anyone else who worked there would not have even opened the door; over the years they were used to his occasional "unusual" methods of treatment.

"Joseph, this is something that I must do. I beg of you, no matter what happens, no matter what you might see or hear, you must not interfere in any way, shape, or form. Understand that if that were to happen you would put not only myself in harm's way but Elena as well," he told Bell, "It is for her that your professional services may soon be needed."

Bell had said nothing, just took a place outside of the design in the corner of the room. The Scotsman extracted a thick cigar from inside his coat pocket but did not light it. Instead, he stood there quietly, brandishing the tobacco like a weapon.

After lighting the candles Van Helsing sat cross-legged in the middle of the design. He tried to push everything else out of his mind, focusing on Elena and the place where she dwelled. A distant carillon marked the half-hour and then the hour as Van Helsing stared down at the Codex pages that he had laid in a semi-circle around him.

He began to read, carefully pronouncing each word, hoping that the impromptu translation would be accurate. Between one heartbeat and the next Van Helsing felt everything change. The asylum was gone, there was no sign of Bell or Elena or even the city.

Van Helsing knew this place; he had walked here and in others like it over the years. At first glance, it seemed like a hill far out in the countryside. Nothing appeared that much out of the ordinary, but no matter what direction he looked in, nothing felt quite right.

Coming toward him from the west was a man dressed in the Bedouin robes of an Arab. The figure never seemed to go faster than a brisk walk, but grew closer at an amazing pace. When the man stopped in front of him, Van Helsing recognized the face, a scarred cheek, hawk-like nose, and eyes that drove themselves into the soul of whatever he looked at. The long mustachios only clinched the identification.

He had met Richard Francis Burton, the knighted translator of the Arabian Nights, on several occasions before the man's death. He could see that face in this younger one that stood in front of him.

"I must say, for a man dead these three years you are definitely looking remarkably healthy, Sir Richard," said Van Helsing.

The figure laughed. It was a sound that sent a chill into Van Helsing's heart. For no more than a moment the human shape was gone, replaced by something else; with tentacles, teeth, half a hundred eyes, and a stench that would have made a freshly dead corpse smell like perfume.

Then the man in the Arab robes stood in front of Van Helsing again. He refused to allow himself to think of this "thing" as the man whose face it wore.

"If you have something to say," said Van Helsing, trying to sound bored, "then let us say it and move on."

"Direct. I like this. Very well, go home," it said. "I could have sent one of my children, but it pleased me to offer fair warning."

"The same way you sent one of them to try to kill my wife?"

The figure laughed and began to speak in a vaguely Arabic dialect, though the words were like nothing heard on the seas of sand.

"Abraham!" Elena's voice cut through the mist. Van Helsing turned toward it.

That very action was enough to shake him loose, he realized, from the holding spell that the thing had on him.

Long tendrils of pulsating flesh were inching their way toward his legs. He kicked at them, driving the toes of his boots into the sod. That seemed to be enough to drive them back, for the moment at least.

"Abraham!" Though he could not see them, Van Helsing felt two hands grabbing his arm and yanking him back into swirling mist. The sensation of falling through a door surrounded him and then everything was calm.

Taking several deep breaths, Van Helsing looked around. Again the scene had changed, but again it was a place that he knew, too damned well. No peaceful landscape this, but ruins that stretched on as far as the eye could see. The night sky was filled with churning clouds that gave the whole place a feeling of never-ending midnight. Cyclopean ruins stretched to the landscape and beyond. What life there might have been here had long since been crushed out.

This was the realm of Yog Sog Oth, the demon beyond the gate, one of the Old Ones, beings locked away from the earth after their reign of terror, who were always struggling to return. To some, they were gods, to others demons, to Van Helsing they had always been something to fear which must never be allowed to escape from their prisons.

A hundred yards in front of him he could see a pair of twin pylons, electricity filling the air between them like a Van der Grif generator gone wild. Van Helsing knew this place all too well. There had not been a day in the last dozen years when the image of it had left his mind. His hand clenched and he could feel the obsidian knife for a moment. She was as he had last seen her, stretched out on an altar-like slab of rock in front of the pylons, her face pale; the wind whipping strands of hair across it. She had not aged in the dozen years since the two of them had arrived in this place, come to place a seal that would keep Yog Sog Oth from coming through the gate.

Why should she age? This was her soul, her true self, as real to the touch as anything, though her true body lay in the asylum, raving about penguins and hurling monkeys. Van Helsing fought down the self-loathing that sought to rise in his throat, with the knowledge that he had condemned the woman he loved to lie as guardian of this place for the rest of her life.

Van Helsing's eyes fell on the dagger, still buried to the hilt in her heart. His fingers clenched with the memory of wrapping themselves around it, the memory of her hands on his, helping to push the blade into her heart.

"No. No," he said and reached out to touch her cold cheek, tears rolling down his face. His hand brushed against the silver swan brooch on her blouse, a gift on their first anniversary.

"Abraham."

Elena stood at his side, a look of sadness and joy in her eyes. Unlike the figure on the alter, who wore a traveling skirt, vest, and loose blouse, this woman wore a gown of black and scarlet, an identical silver swan brooch affixed to her left breast, her face young and not yet touched by pain and madness.

Van Helsing reached for her but she pulled back just out of his reach. "I'm sorry, Abraham. What you see is at best an echo of what I was. Over the eternity since we first set foot in this hellhole, I've learned to tap some of the power in the pylons. That's what has let me reach out to you, to pull you back from the Codex and away from that thing that sought to stop you."

"I know, my darling. You are always looking out for me. But now I've come to free you, Elena. There is a way," he said.

The look of sadness deepened in Elena's eyes, mixed with a way fear. "I know that was what you said you would try to do. But we both know it cannot be. I have become one with this place, and it was necessary for a human soul from a still-living body to hold the line here."

"It should have been me," said Van Helsing.

"It could not," she answered softly. "Of the two of us, only you had the knowledge and skill to make it work. That is why I guided your hand when…"

"I drove the dagger into your heart," he said bitterly. "Now I've come up with a way that you can walk out of the asylum. For all these years I've searched for a way. I knew there had to be one, and I've found it."

"No, Abraham, you know that cannot be, no matter how much either one of us wants it. The gate can only be held as long as there is a guardian, one whose soul is imprisoned here and whose body lives on Earth. You said so yourself," she reminded him. "In the eternity since that moment I've come to know the truth of your words. Besides, with the terror that has held, that has pounded into the very core of my soul I do not believe I would be able to wear sanity again."

The seals on the gate had worn away with the passing millennia. Only the willing sacrifice of someone to become the guardian could keep them in place.

"No, I will not permit it to be so," screamed Van Helsing. "One of the followers of Nyarlathotep tried to kill you tonight. I do not know what I would have done had he succeeded."

"You would have gone on, sadder, but you would have gone on to face each dawn as you have all your life. I would give anything to stand with you again, facing the unknown, growing old at your side. But that cannot be. I know that what happened will happen again, as surely as one day follows another. The followers of the Elder Gods are always probing, trying to find ways to free their deities," she said.

"No, Elena, I am your husband. I know what is best for you," he told her, feeling more determined than ever.

"As I know that you must not do this. There is a great evil that will soon be afoot in the world. The only way it can be defeated is if you are there to hold the line and drive it back." Waves of images flashed in Van Helsing's mind: wolves, a woman dressed in a gossamer gown, an aristocratic man standing in the turret of a castle, fog, and death flowing everywhere.

Van Helsing looked toward the echo of his wife. She had moved away from him and the altar. Elena's arms were raised above her head, partially blocking her face. From her open palms shot bolts of light, glowing a sickly green that flew outwards faster than anything he had ever seen.

They struck him, hitting his chest with the force of a horse's hoof, wrapping around him as an ever-tightening vine. Van Helsing staggered backward, one arm free and frantically struggling to balance himself with it.

"My darling, our paths are different now; they always will be," she said, tears rolling down her face. "You must go back. Remember that I love you and will always be near."

Van Helsing felt words dying in his throat as he rolled through a door into darkness. The last image before he passed out was the silver swan pin, one on the woman standing in front of him and one as his hand closed around it.

"You had no intention of coming back, did you?"

Van Helsing stared into the amber liquid that half-filled his brandy snifter for several moments before he finally took a swallow. He had never particularly liked the taste of brandy, preferring the taste of a good single malt. But in this case, the burning sensation as it rolled down his throat felt very right.

I didn't surprise him that Bell had divined his plans, though for a time he had hardly admitted to himself what he would have had to do to actually bring "Elena" back. The gate could not be left without a guardian. The lack of one was what had precipitated problems in the first place.

"Do I take it now that you have had an encounter at the crossroads and become a believer?" he asked Bell.

"I'm hardly Saul of Tarsus. As I said, I believe that you believe, and you believed that you could expiate the guilt you felt over Elena's condition by exchanging places with her." Bell was standing near a large globe, idly running the fingers of his left hand over continent after continent as they rotated in the wrong direction.

"That sounds like a bit of reasoning that that fellow from Vienna would follow," said Van Helsing.

"Freud, you mean?"

"Yes, that's the fellow. I can imagine he would class me in with some of those rather colorfully named patients of his. But, getting back to you, I suppose you can supply me with one of those eminently obvious line of reasoning to back up your conclusion," he said.

"Actually, in this case, it was a lot simpler. Before leaving England, I had Lee Satterfield take a look at those parchments. She gave me a rough idea of what they said. Seems that the spell you were wanting to make work, required an exchange, one for another," said Bell. "Knowing how you blame yourself for what happened to Elena, the rest was obvious."

"Very good, old friend. It would have worked, too," Van Helsing said, his voice a harsh whisper. "Except she fought me, wanted to remain in that hellish place." He wanted to say more, to let his pain rage out, the frustration he felt at having failed the woman that he loved.

"Abraham, I wish to the depths of my being that I had some scientific trick, some magic wand to wave; that would take away the pain that you are feeling. That I could prove to you it was all in your mind. But I know that to you it was very real," said Bell.

Van Helsing reached into his pocket and brought out the silver swan pin. It had been real, very real. When he had awakened on the floor of Elena's room it had been clutched in his hand, hard enough to cut into the palm.

"Do you plan to try again?"

Van Helsing shook his head. "No. Elena said that my place was here, that there was great evil that I had to confront. Lord knows what she was talking about." As he spoke, Van Helsing picked up the pile of mail that had accumulated on his desk. At the bottom was a letter bearing an English stamp and postmark. He opened it and half-heartedly scanned the contents.

"Joseph, when do you plan to return to Scotland?"

"I have to be back in two weeks. I was planning on leaving this Friday."

"Good. That will be just enough time to put matters in order here. I hope that you will not object to some company, at least part way."

"Indeed not," said Bell. "May I ask why the sudden desire to travel to England?"

Van Helsing held up the letter. "This is from a former student of mine, John Seward. He operates an asylum near Whitby, outside of London. There is a case there he needs to consult me on."

"Excellent. A visit to the English countryside will do you a world of good."

## The End

# ELEVEN TO SEVEN SHIFT

The drug pump ticked steadily away, like an old hand-wound pocket watch. Sam Larson looked up from his newspaper, eyed the dispenser, and then checked his watch.

It had been just under ten minutes since the light on the dispenser had shifted to red. When it shifted to green, in just under a minute, it would mean another dose of Demerol was available.

Mark Larson, Sam's eighty-year-old father, stirred in the hospital bed. He had been sleeping on and off since early morning, but rarely for more than an hour or two at a time.

Sam drew a deep breath. He wanted to do something, anything, to alleviate his father's pain. But all he, or any of the rest of the family, could do was sit there and hit the pain medication button every ten minutes. Oh, the drug helped; there was no doubt about that. It was just that Sam felt like there ought to be something more that he could do.

The family had been there for two days. No, it was closer to three, he realized.

Thankfully, Debbie, Sam's wife, and his cousin Karen had managed to convince his mother to go home around 9:30. Otherwise the stubborn older woman would have remained at her husband's bedside twenty-four hours a day.

"Mom, you need the rest. Go home. I'll stay with him," Sam had told his mother. "And don't try and say that I should go home and rest; you need it worse than I do. You may be stubborn and hard-headed, but remember, I get it from both you and Dad. So no matter what, I'll win."

She had laughed and hugged him. "I want you to know," she said, "that you are picking on your old decrepit mother. Is that any way for a loyal son to act?"

"Mom, you are neither old nor decrepit, and I've heard that line from you since I was two or three years old. Don't you think it's time that you got some new material?"

He'd promised them he would stay only a couple more hours. Right now this was where he needed to be, for himself as much as for his father's needing him.

Sam turned toward the bed.

It had been early Friday morning, just after six, when they had followed his parents' car on a round-about route to Northwest Memorial Hospital.

"It will be all right," Debbie said.

Sam desperately hoped so. After a lot of effort to save it, the doctor advised amputation of the lower part of Mark Larson's leg as the only remaining course. A history of bad circulation, infection, and several strokes had made it inevitable.

"It was either this, or the next thing would have been gangrene, and that would have killed him," Sam's mother had said. "The doctor told us everything and then left it up to your Dad. He thought it over for twenty-four hours. It was his decision to make."

The operation had gone well, only about forty-five minutes and they had him in recovery. Another half hour and he was awake and on the way to a room.

Sam rested his elbow on the chair's arm. At least these were more comfortable than those hard plastic and metal things in the surgical waiting room. Whoever had designed them didn't seem to understand the concept of comfort.

The wall behind the hospital bed was crisscrossed with shadows. Familiar shapes, bed railings, chairs, and a dresser, were all twisted and formed into other outsized shapes by the light coming from the small safety light built into the wall near the floor.

For a long time, Sam just sat there, watching the shadows, listening to the pump's sound, half hearing the innumerable hospital sounds that drifted in through the partially closed door.

Yet with a precision edge honed by exhaustion, he never missed the scheduled time for the drug button.

"You know, you're not doing him any good if you run yourself into the ground."

A small red-haired woman stood on the other side of the bed. She wore a blue surgical scrub uniform, a laminated ID badge clipped to one corner. It took Sam several seconds to focus his eyes enough to read her name: Kara Allison LPN.

"How many times a week do you end up having to give that kind of advice?"

"Maybe five or six at the most." She began to check his father's pulse, first at his wrist and then on the left foot. Sam watched her ever so gently hold a stethoscope against the sleeping man's chest.

"Not checking the blood pressure?" Sam asked.

"No need to wake him up right now. I think he's going to sleep pretty well for the rest of the night. Everything else looks pretty good, considering what he's been through." She picked up the spiral chart notebook lying on a nearby table and began to make notes in it.

"I'm glad to hear that. It's been a rough couple of days," Sam said. "Is it pronounced Care-a?"

"That's right."

Sam stared at her for a long time. The girl seemed to blend into the darkness, all but her eyes. They seemed to pull what little light there was in the room into them, reflecting it back in a silver haze.

"I haven't seen you here before," he said. "Have you been working the eleven to seven shift long?"

"Sometimes it seems too long," she sighed. "But I work where I have to, where I'm needed. At least it's a job."

They say that sometimes the human mind can make great intuitive leaps if it's put under the right stress, the right set of pressures. At that moment Sam did that and all traces of exhaustion fell away from him.

"I think that we've met before, haven't we?" he asked.

"Really? This isn't going to be a pickup line now, is it? You know that in spite of what you saw in all those old Roger Corman drive-in movies, all nurses aren't horny and easy."

"No, it's definitely not a pickup line. I wouldn't try to pick you up."

"Really?" Kara said, sounding slightly offended. "That's what they all say. At least you have the class not to try and secretly slip your wedding ring off."

Sam ran his finger along the edge of his wedding ring; the grooves that made up the Hopi design in it were sharp and prominent.

"No, I really don't think that it would be a good idea to try and seriously put any moves on Death."

Kara made a final notation on the chart and returned it to the bedside table. Sam thought he heard a soft sensuous chuckle.

"Death? Me? I have to wonder, Sam, if you may have been helping yourself to some of your father's medication. I imagine in the right amounts it might be fun. You should have at least offered to share. Who knows, it might have gotten you somewhere?"

"No, I doubt that. No drugs. Just a feeling of certainty that I had seen you before. At fires, at wrecks, that sort of thing. The faces are different, but that glow in your eyes; it's always the same.

Kara pushed a loose hair back behind her left ear. "You're something pretty special, Mr. Larson. I've heard a lot of fantasies and been the subject of my share of propositions, but this is an entirely new one."

"So I'm wrong, am I?"

"What do you think?"

"Maybe, maybe not. If I am, then you can just put this down to the raving of a patient's exhausted son," Sam said.

Only he knew he was right. The feeling in his gut had hardened into certainty with each passing moment. Sam stood up and walked around the bed, to face Kara with only the standard hospital issue wheeled table between them.

"Now, if I were who you think I am, why do you think I would be here?"

"Don't try to talk to me like I'm an idiot," Sam said gently. "You also don't have to worry, if I'm wrong, about me maybe trying to do something physical."

"That's a relief," she said. "Then let's talk about this. I've got a few minutes. If I am Death, and I'm not claiming that, am I here for him?" as she gestured toward the bed.

"That's what I think."

"Or maybe am I here for you? You smoke too much, work too hard, are stressed out to the max, and haven't really relaxed since you were around eight years old."

Sam stared at her. A cold breeze wrapped itself around his gut. Every word that she had said was dead on accurate.

"So how do you know all this about me?"

"Well, I could be, as you suspect, Death itself and therefore know everything. Or on the other hand, I could just be extremely observant and able to make some good guesses. You know, the way that Sherlock Holmes did."

"If it's me that you've come for, I won't resist. That's fine. But if you're here for him, then I guess we may have to tangle about it," he said.

There was a long silence between them wrapped in the echoing of a gurney being pushed past the door.

"No, son."

Mark Larson had raised himself on his elbow, the light playing over his pale face.

"Dad, relax, you need to rest. Try to go back to sleep. Leave this to me," Sam said, hearing the slight tremor in his own voice as he spoke.

"No. I've been awake for a while and heard what you've been saying. I know how crazy it sounds, but if you're right, then there isn't a damn thing that either one of us can do about it."

"Dad, I can't let you go like this. Not if there's a chance to change things. You always said a man takes care of his family. I saw you do that quietly every day I was growing up. You never said a lot, you just did it. Now it's my turn."

The older man smiled. "Sam, you've got a lot more ahead of you than I could possibly have ahead of me. If she's come for me, then it's best that you let me go. You don't think I wouldn't want to spend another fifty years with your mother, provided she could put up with me, do you?

"But at least this way the pain will be stopped. It's been ten years since I wasn't in some kind of pain. There are times it hurt so much that I've found myself praying to die," Mark Larson said.

"I know, Dad, I know. It's driven me crazy seeing you like that and wishing I could do something about it."

"I'm proud of you for what you're trying to do."

Sam smiled. It helped to hear those words. He knew his father had always been proud of him, but Mark was the kind of man who rarely said things about how he felt. He reached over and took his father's hand, squeezing it tightly. For the first time in a long time, he felt the old strength in his father's hand.

"Kara," he said to the redhead. "You're just going to have to take me as well if you want him."

She stared at them both, her silver eyes lighting up the room.

"You've got a hell of a son there, Mr. Larson," she said as she leaned forward and kissed Mark on the cheek. "I suspect that he takes after his old man. Listen, I think you two guys have got a lot of talking to do, so I better be getting along."

Before either man could speak, Kara turned and headed for the door.

"See you around sometime, fellows," she said sensually.

Kara Allison stood in the hospital snack bar and studied the soda machine. Four of the seven offerings glowed red, i.e.: empty. The remaining selection was none too appealing. Well, what did she expect, Kara reminded herself, the wine list at the Ritz Carlton, especially at 2 a.m.?

With a sigh, she began to search through her pocket for some change.

What she retrieved was a yo-yo, many pieces of scrap paper, and a crumpled-up chewing gum package. Wrapped up inside the latter, however, were two quarters and a buffalo head nickel.

This wasn't the first time she'd been recognized. It wouldn't be the last. Only, in this case, being recognized was the whole reason she was there in the first place.

There were other things that she did besides her established duties; other things that affected people for good or ill.

Oh, she'd be back for Mark Larson in the not-very-distant future. His son would join her for a walk eventually, as well. But for now, they had a chance, a chance to really talk. That was important.

Kara smiled, shoving the quarters into the machine. For less than a heartbeat, she allowed herself to morph into what most people would have considered her traditional form, as a skeleton hand pushed the button for Diet Pepsi, caffeine-free, of course.

## The End

# BACK IN THE "REAL WORLD"

A lean dark figure, dressed in a leather flight jacket, black jeans, and boots, had the badge of an Oklahoma State Park ranger pinned on his shirt. Will Jared had spent a half hour studying a campsite. He knelt on one knee, next to the remains of the campfire. The ashes had been there three days, perhaps as many as five.

Ordinary park visitors probably, but there was always a chance of something else. That was what had drawn Jared here.

This late in October campers were not unknown in this part of northeast Oklahoma, just unusual. Most people preferred an electric blanket to a plastic ground sheet and a sleeping bag. Plus, most campers who used Hyatt State Park registered with the park ranger's office.

There were always a few who didn't bother.

Jared was justly proud of his tracking skills. He'd learned from the best, his maternal grandfather, Marcus Conley, who was said to have been one of the best Cherokee hunting guides in decades. What Grandfather hadn't taught Jared, six years in the United States Army Rangers had.

He took a handful of ashes, rolling them between his palms. Then he gently blew his breath and the ash lingered as mist in the cold night air.

*It* began slowly as it had so many times since his return to "The Real World" from Vietnam, three years before. The sounds of the forest became distant and faint, overlaid with other sounds, vague echoes that grew gradually into voices.

*I know this isn't the sort of honeymoon that you expected. It's ... just ... that ...*

*I don't care. I'm here with* **you**, *we're together. That's all that counts. Us.*

Honeymooners?! Of course, it made sense with the other signs he had seen in the area. Just people who wanted to be left by themselves; a sentiment that Jared could very easily identify with. Being alone was one of the main reasons he had taken the job as a park ranger.

There were more words, words that gradually faded into other sounds. Jared struggled to pull himself away from them. It was difficult not to let himself go, to let the echoing sounds of voices, the wind, the trees, and the very soil itself just pull him into them.

He could feel rightness about it. So easy, so very easy to let go and let it envelop him. Only not this way. Gradually that certainty brought him to himself, the odors of pine, grass, and water growing around him.

Jared's hands were trembling as the gray ashes fell slowly between his fingers. A breeze brought the distant sound of an owl screeching.

When everything around him began to move, Jared grabbed the limb of a nearby sapling to balance himself. He pulled his flight jacket tighter. *Afterward,* Jared always felt like he had been dumped in a freezer.

There were probably reasons to explain the reaction; there always were. Jared often suspected that they made as little sense to the people giving them as to the people hearing them.

But Jared knew better than to mention this to the chief ranger, a bureaucrat from the word go. This was the sort of thing that would convince him that Will Jared had gone round the bend.

Once, and only once, Jared had tried to describe the experience to the doctors at the Veterans Administration hospital in Tulsa. They had listened, muttering phrases like *"survivor' guilt," "delayed stress syndrome,"* and *"fear trauma."* Their answer had been yet another prescription, which, like the others, had disappeared into the waiting-room trash can.

When he told his grandfather about the voices and the rest, Marcus Conley didn't say much. The old man had just sat on the porch, listening and puffing away on his pipe, surrounding himself with clouds of Jameson blend tobacco smoke.

"You're not crazy, boy. You just have to wait. You got the potential to be something very special, for yourself, and for our people. But you've got demons you've got to face, inside yourself, like every one of us. Only, yours are tougher, harder, and more devious. And you can't pick the time to face them, they pick it, and you just have to do the best you can."

"Yeah, right," Jared said.

The wind came from the west, off the lake, and into the narrow valley, the chill in it was a stark contrast to the last remnants of summer that had clung to the area until only a half dozen days before.

Jared came down along the hillside, pausing here and there to look and listen.

The nearest neighbors were a good three miles away, closer on the shoreline, near the park's edge.

He fumbled through his jacket pockets and pulled out a pack of Camels, along with a Zippo lighter. Its brass surface was scarred and bent, but not enough to obscure the engraving: KHE SANH 1969.

Thumbing the lighter to life, he sucked on the cigarette, its smoke burning harshly as he drew deep on it.

Jared smothered a cough in his sleeve, and fought to hold himself up as it racked his body. He told himself that .it was just the tag end of a summer cold, but it had held on for nearly two months. Maybe it wouldn't be such a bad idea to visit the tribal medical complex near Tahlequah, or maybe the V.A. Hospital, for a checkup.

No, if he went to Tahlequah that would mean the obligatory visit to his parents. It was never a pleasant task, not since the morning he had walked into the house and announced that he had enlisted in the Army.

Going back to the V.A. didn't appeal to him, either. Not because of the doctors. That had been where he had his first flashback; one minute he'd been in Tulsa, the next in 'Nam. He shook his head; no V.A. Besides, there were probably too many new forms to fill out if he went in.

Jared glanced across the clearing. Even knowing where to look, it was still hard to see the cabin in the dark. *All the better,* he told himself. *If I have trouble seeing it, others do too.*

The cabin seemed to fit here as if it had always been a part of the forest. It was set against the side of a hill, and a dozen small ash trees surrounded it. In the years since they had been planted, the trees had grown much larger than anyone would have expected.

Lingering on the porch, Jared partially unzipped his flight jacket. His hand rested on the butt of the silver-gray Deutonics .45, waiting. When at last he was certain there was no one else around, Jared stepped inside.

Dropping his jacket on the couch, Jared drew a deep breath, savoring the warmth of the house. The cabin had three rooms: kitchen and living area combined bedroom with bath, and a storage area. Small it might be, but that summer after graduation when he, Larry Sheppard, and Larry's father had sweated, struggled, and cursed to build it, the cabin had seemed as big as an Alpine A-frame. Originally, they had intended it for an occasional getaway. Since Jared had come back from 'Nam to "The Real World," it had been home and refuge for him.

That was when he remembered the ice cream. A half gallon of homemade chocolate chip, carefully packed and handed to him by his mother on his last visit to his parents' home. Yeah, that was exactly the prescription, the sort the V.A. doctors *should* be writing. He filled a big bowl, helping himself to several large bites in the process, then carried it into the living room.

Spooning a mouthful of ice cream, Jared found himself staring at the scar across the palm of his right hand. With the edge of a fingernail he carefully traced the line. That had come from a screwdriver slipping out of his grip. It had hurt but the memory didn't anymore.

The summer they had built the cabin had been special, very special for Larry and him. They had been best friends almost from the first day at the Cherokee boarding school near Lawton. That summer, nine years ago, they had become in formal ceremony what they were already in fact: brothers.

A blood brother was always there, always ready when you needed him.

Only, when push came to shove, I wasn't there when Larry really needed me.

Jared repeated it over and over again in his mind, like a Gregorian chant.

I wasn't there. I wasn't there.

On the table next to the divan was a framed photo of the two of them in Class A uniforms, taken the week they had arrived in Vietnam: perfectly ironed shirts, spit-shined boots, a dream image as far from the reality as Jared wished he were now.

He picked up the picture, his slim brown fingers tightening around the metal.

*... tell the truth, you broke your ankle when her husband was coming home and you had to dive out the window.*

*Right! You know without me at point you couldn't find your way out of a one-room schoolhouse.*

*Sure! Just stay here, recuperate on the beach, with all these nice army nurses to look after you while the real men are out working.*

*My Friend, it's hard duty but that's what they pay me the big bucks for.*

*I'm sorry, Lt. Jared, they found what was left of the patrol. Charlie hit Sheppard and the rest of them hard, about five klicks from the LZ...No survivors...*

Jared *listened* for a long time, the sounds holding him tight, yanking

...found himself staring at the scar...

the very breath out of his body. As swiftly as it had begun, everything ended in a wave of pain, like someone slamming a fist into his stomach. He rammed the photo down on the table, jarring the bowl of half-eaten ice cream onto the floor.

As his fingers parted from the metal, Jared found himself watching the whole scene with a disinterested eye, coldly picking out details that echoed loudly in his vision.

For a long time he just sat there, staring at the fire, the puddle of melting ice cream and broken glass. Struggling to his feet, Jared finally began to pick up the pieces; it just didn't seem right to leave them there.

The drumming awoke Jared. He had been aware of it for a long time, hoping the whole thing was part of a dream that would run its course and go on to something different.

Half-heartedly, Jared buried his face in the pillow, but he knew as he rolled to one side that it would do no good. He forced his eyes open, looking toward the digital display on the bedside clock.

**3:45**.

"Damn!"

As he stepped onto the cabin's porch a few moments later, the night chill cut through him. For a long time, he just walked, boots lost in the knee-high ground fog.

The wind did sometimes play funny tricks in the hills. He could remember nights during the summer when you could hear sounds coming from the far side of the lake as easily as if they had been next door. Only tonight there wasn't any wind.

"Too much chocolate-chip ice cream will do it to you every time, kiddo." The voice came from just ahead of him, as did the drumming.

Sitting cross-legged on a lightning-blackened stump was an old man, dressed in jeans and a Grateful Dead T-shirt. He had a small drum on his lap. The man's shoulder-length gray hair was held in place by an ornately beaded hair tie, the kind that Jared had seen some of the tribal elders wear.

"Do you take requests?" Jared said.

The old man looked up and smiled, produced a Scottish pennywhistle, and began to play. The tune was familiar. It took a moment or two before Jared could put a name to it, "As Time Goes By."

After he finished, the old man looked at Jared, raising the whistle in a salute.

"I really don't think that anybody is going to mistake you for Dooley Wilson," Jared said.

The old man shrugged.

"Does this mean I should call you Sam?"

"Up to you. I answer to a lot of things."

And Jared knew him.

He couldn't say just what wild leap of logic suddenly told him just who "Sam" was; it just happened. "In this day and age, it sounds a little more suitable than calling you Coyote."

Sam nodded, a look of satisfaction on his face. "Not bad; you're quicker on things than I'd been told." The fog began to move in a slow circular motion around the two men.

That was when Sam changed. He was younger, closer to Jared's age. A few white hairs streaked the man's otherwise ink-black hair. He now wore a gray sports jacket, sunglasses, purple shirt, and an outlandish paisley neckerchief. The drum was replaced by a saxophone.

Sam produced a white handkerchief from his jacket sleeve and began to polish the instrument. When he had finished, Sam pulled the reed loose and held it up for a closer look. The edges were visibly cracked and worn. With a flourish, he flung the reed off into the darkness, produced another one, and fit it into place.

"You know, boy, I'm sure beginning to wonder if you're really worth the amount of *my* time that you've taken up," he said.

"Well, excuse me! I don't seem to recall asking for your time or your attention. I think I was doing just fine without you sticking your nose into my affairs. And even if I did need help, I'm not sure I would want *yours*," Jared said.

Anger flared on Sam's face. "Look, boy, in spite of what you may have heard, I'm not nearly the interfering bastard as I've been played up over the years. Let's just say that I've gotten a lot of bad press and leave it at that." He began to play, this time a tune that Jared did not recognize.

"Would you mind doing your rehearsing somewhere else? There are a few people around here who want to sleep."

"Well, pardon me," Sam answered with mock indignation. At that moment he was once more the old man, though the saxophone was still gripped tightly in his hands. "Besides, that's not the way you were taught to address someone. Now was it?"

Jared suppressed a feeling of irritation. Sam was correct and that bothered him.

By tribal custom, one should address an older man as either uncle or grandfather, whether you were related or not. It was just good manners, as well as a sign of respect; if he truly were Coyote, this Sam's age alone gave him claim to the title.

Jared turned to walk away, shivering, as Sam began playing again. The sound echoed around him, even louder than before. The sudden desire for a cigarette filled him. The problem was, he realized almost at once that the cigarettes and his lighter were back in the cabin.

The fog had grown so heavy that Jared could barely see more than a half-dozen steps in front of him. It was difficult to even make out the numbers on his watch.

3:48

Three minutes? That hardly seemed possible. It was getting more and more difficult to know what to believe standing there at the center of a moving whirlwind of fog, color, motion, and sound.

The smell of burning diesel and gas filled his lungs. People sped by on foot, in rickshaws, on motorcycles, and in cars; voices chattered in French, Vietnamese, Thai, American, a dozen dialects and a hundred combinations, all melding into one voice.

Saigon.

He knew where he was, although at that particular moment he would not have been willing to bet that the sun would rise in the east tomorrow morning.

Saigon.

Not the pale gray echo called Ho Chi Minh City. It could be no other place but Saigon, in all its decadence and glory.

Jared drew a breath, held it, and then slowly exhaled. He wasn't sure if he wanted this to be a bizarre nightmare or an even more bizarre reality.

A small gray cat, missing a single fang, emerged from an alley and hopped up on the packing crate in front of Jared. The animal eyed him for nearly a minute, seeming to dare Jared to walk past, then began ever so calmly to bathe itself.

"You here to tell me something? I'm open for suggestions." He felt kind of silly talking to the cat, but at the moment it seemed.\ the thing to do.

"Would you listen if I did?" the cat said.

"That tears it," Jared mumbled. "I'm outta here."

Half walking, half jogging, Jared moved in and out among the constant flow of people and vehicles, moving from shadow to light and back again. After a half hour, he found himself on more residential streets, where most of the houses reflected the architecture of thirty and forty years before.

That was when a trio of U.S. Army half-ton trucks came around the comer. The glare from their headlights made it impossible to see the drivers' faces as they passed.

The final one had no tailgate. On impulse, Jared ran after it, boosting himself onto the back with no problem. Scooting inside, he wrapped himself in the steamy darkness. The engine roared and the truck pulled ahead.

Just a place to rest, a chance to think, that was all he wanted. For a moment the image of himself wrapped in a straightjacket, screaming his throat raw in some V.A. padded cell, lingered in his mind, mixed with the quiet face of his grandfather.

A few moments later he was lost in sleep.

Jared was jolted awake when the truck hit a rut in the road. The stiffness in his shoulders and back was painful testimony to how much time had passed. The truck continued to barrel along at a good clip as Jared crouched on the back edge before stepping off into the darkness. He barely managed to stay on his feet when he landed.

The sky was awash in stars. Around him, the night sounds of the jungle abounded. Beads of sweat rolled down his neck to stain his shirt and the fur collar of his flight jacket.

Carefully he picked a path among the bushes and vines. As he walked, the jungle noises around him began to fade. Not quickly, but over a period of time, until there was nothing, no wind, no animal noises, no annoying buzz of insects. Nothing, except the sounds of his own steps.

Jared's foot was almost on top of the booby trap when he spotted the first Viet Cong.

A tripwire wrapped in vines had been strung about five inches above the ground, hooked to a claymore mine that would have peppered him with shrapnel if he had set it off.

"Just be a bit more careful. Somebody who's been in country all of thirty minutes would have spotted this," he told himself, stepping over the wire.

The guerrilla fighter, on the other hand, was a good twenty yards in front of Jared, with his back to him. Bent low, the man wore black homespun and clutched a Russian AK-47 in his hands. Jared's hand began to slowly loosen the heavy, hand-tooled belt he wore. Garroting someone with your cowboy belt might not have much style, but it would do in a pinch.

Only, this guy didn't seem to notice Jared. As the young man got closer, the VC didn't look around, didn't move, and gave every appearance of being frozen solid. Jared moved up beside him and just stood there, staring. After several minutes, he might have seen the other man's chest move, but couldn't be sure.

Just ahead and to his right, Jared spotted more figures. Some were VC, the rest were North Vietnamese regulars. All of them were standing as stone still as the first.

That was when he spotted Larry.

His blood brother had an M-16 balanced in the crook of his arm, freeing his hands up to examine a map. Next to him were two faces that Jared knew well, Corporals Kelley Wilde and Hal Williams.

Like the VC and the North Vietnamese regulars, they were frozen in mid-movement.

For several long minutes, Jared just stared. This time he was sure he saw one of Wilde's arms move, ever so slightly. If they *could* see him he suspected all they would notice would be a shadow, a vague movement out of the corner of one eye.

Just to one side was the rest of the squad: Matt Charles, Jim Allen, Bill Gordon, Jonas Mason, Karl Tattershall, and K.T. Dixon. Gordon and Dixon were carrying a makeshift litter, with Charles stretched across it, a heavy bandage across the man's chest. All of the men bore wounds of some kind.

"They must have been in one hell of a firefight."

Something hit Jared hard, driving him to the ground. He managed to roll to one side, grabbing handfuls of grass as he did. Pulling to his feet, Jared found himself facing not a VC or NVA regular, but someone wearing American-issue combat fatigues. Dog tags glittered in the moonlight, hanging loose on the man's chest, and a bandanna covered most of his face.

"Hey, bro. I'm one of the good guys," Jared stammered.

The newcomer didn't hear or seem to care. Pulling a knife from his boot he advanced toward Jared.

Using his left hand, Jared began to slowly whirl his best around. Moving in concert with the other man, he never let his eyes lose contact with the stranger's.

They both struck at one, Jared driving the heavy metal buckle hard against the head of the other man, who skillfully jabbed the knife as he tried to duck away. The blade's razor-sharp edge slid across Jared's side, cutting the leather and flesh.

He'd been cut before, but this was different. The pain stung like nothing he had ever experienced, tearing through every fiber of his body. The other man managed to land several good kicks that sent Jared collapsing into a crouch on the ground.

Reality began to fragment. Jared felt his body being pulled apart. Muscle and sinew rolled in waves, ripping and splitting and melding through a dozen, a hundred new forms. Every time he tried to scream his voice was lost in waves of pain that seemed like they would never end.

And it was over.

Jared pulled his hands up to his face, only what he saw weren't hands, but fur-covered paws. The claws of a great brown bear faced him. A bear's growl tore out of his throat.

Jared turned to face his opponent. From somewhere the man had produced an M-16 and had it at his shoulder ready to fire. With a single swipe of a huge paw, the bear/Jared knocked it from the man's hand, sending his opponent flying to the ground.

Then the bear was gone.

Jared felt his muscles and bones ripping and tearing, again, shifting in an intricate jigsaw puzzle. With the brushing of wind across them, they began to re-form. Jared felt *himself* step away from his body. There was pain, but he accepted it, allowing the sensation to become something distant and not part of him.

A screaming falcon flapped its wings in anger above the prone form of Jared's enemy. It would have been so easy to let go, let the bird or the bear rip this man apart. So easy.

"NO!"

The voice was enough to bring Jared back. The falcon faded but did not disappear entirely. It merged into the background, standing with the bear. The part of him that was Will Jared had found a balance, an uneasy one, between the man, the animals, and the earth itself. He held on to it for all that he was worth.

Kneeling next to the other man, Jared grabbed the discarded knife, pushing it against the man's throat.

"If you move, if you even blink wrong, I'll gut you like a fish.

You understand?"

The man nodded.

Jared pulled the bandanna away. The face that stared back at him was covered in camouflage makeup and dirt. He knew the face, it was his own.

"Hi, guy!"

"I should kill you."

"Go ahead, but somehow I don't think you've got the guts."

"What are you?"

"Oh, give me a break. You know as well as I do. I'm you. Without all that crap and sentimental junk, you've carried around for years. From your folks. From your grandfather. I wasn't born in Oklahoma. I was born right here in 'Nam, for one reason, and that is to survive. I'll kill anybody it takes to do it."

"Even me or Larry?"

"Of course, you! I'd do it in a minute and laugh the whole time. Larry ... that little piss-ant, if he got in my way I'd crush him under my boot, just like any jungle bug. Why do you think I'm here? A little post-mission recon; maybe tie up a few loose ends; maybe change things. Now don't go and tell me that that idea hasn't crossed your mind more than once. You haven't got the balls to do anything about it. When you come down to it, this is nothing more than a matter of plain old simple revenge."

Revenge? For his pain and guilt, for his failure to be there for the man who was his brother. Sure, the thought had crossed Jared's mind, more often than he cared to admit. "Maybe that's what you came here for, but I'm not the one flat on his back with a knife at his throat."

"Then just push it in and get this over with. You are beginning to bore me."

Jared pushed the blade a fraction of an inch. The single drop of blood that appeared around the metal tip revolted him.

"Oh, no you don't. I've got the guts, more than you have, 'friend.' I could kill you, but I don't *need* to. You're a part of me, that I admit, one I don't like, but one that I can live with."

Without even knowing that he wanted to, Jared could feel himself reaching out, not to one object, as he had before, but to everything. Instead of fading, the jungle began to glow with a dim phosphorescence that filled the area.

At one moment, Jared was one with Larry, the squad members, the Vietnamese hidden in the bushes, the trees, the vines, and the very soil. It was all one, separate and unique but still one, and he was a part of it.

He could feel the grass growing under his boots, a monkey poised to leap from branch to branch, the fear that hung heavy on the heart of his blood brother, the men in his squad, and even the Vietnamese they faced.

Everything fitted into a proper place here, it all made sense.

Everything human, animal, and plant had its place, a place to live and a place to die.

Tears rolled down his face as Jared turned toward the glowing form of his blood brother. This was Larry's place to die. Just as Jared would have his own place someday when it was time to move on.

The light faded and he looked around. His other self was gone, back into the shadows.

Jared knew the answer as he looked around. But he had to try anyway, one last time. He owed himself, as well as Larry, that much.

For more than an hour, he examined every angle, played out every possibility, every scenario that he had conceived of over the years; anything that, even in his wildest, most demented imaginings, might have brought the men home. In the end, he had the answer, had known it from the moment that they had brought word of his friend's death.

Part of him wanted to pry the weapon out of someone's hand and just start firing. Only, that would do no good. Jared knew that as certainly as he knew his own name.

He walked up beside Larry, laying his hand on the shoulder of his oldest friend. "I'll see ya when I see ya, buddy."

As the fog began to swirl around him Will Jared was certain that he could smell the distinctive odor of Jameson's blend tobacco.

Jared ran his finger along the edge of the dish. There was just enough chocolate sauce and melted vanilla ice cream left for one final taste.

"One must have the proper respect and consideration for chocolate," he said grinning.

Jared couldn't remember the last time he had felt so relaxed, so free. He had even locked away the Deutonics; anything he was afraid of now, Jared knew he could handle.

Drawing a deep breath, he reached out with his mind, feeling, things around him, the wind, the water, the earth itself, animals moving among the trees and through the water, easily becoming a, part of them, letting them become a part of him

Jared didn't understand everything, even though it all seemed to make a weird sort of sense. He had some vacation time accumulated, and with the holidays coming up it might not be a bad idea to visit his family in

Tahlequah. He could say it was also a trip to visit the tribal medical facility as well. He still had the cough; it wasn't near as bad now, but it wouldn't hurt to get it looked at.

And as long as he was there, a trip to his grandfather's ranch just outside of town, down along the river, and a long talk with the old man would definitely be in order.

For a long time, he stood watching the glow on the eastern horizon. The wind had shifted out of the south, bringing with it the heady smell of the lake and something else, the faint sound of a lone musician playing.

Saxophone music?

Logic said that it was more than likely someone's radio. Jared knew differently; there were times when logic did not apply. Or perhaps it did. He smiled and spoke to the wind. "Thank you, grandfather."

## The End

# EVERYTHING AND NOTHING

A single white rose grew in the soft earth next to the building, its roots digging into the ground and holding tightly. The lanky figure extended a slim pale hand, wrapped in fingerless black leather gloves, to touch its soft petals and savored each bit of the flower, drawing it into himself for just a moment. A single tear ran across his face. Then the rose was alone in the darkness of the alley.

Gideon had been staring at the bonsai tree for fifteen minutes before he finally picked up the small set of clippers. Ever so carefully he began to make precise cuts; sometimes just the barest fraction of a leaf, other times whole pieces of branch.

He had been growing and training bonsai trees for fifteen years, much to Magda's amusement. When they had first met she had dubbed his hobby Zen tree surgery.

"Hey what can I say? It relaxes me," Gideon said.

"I suppose it's better than having you watching Monday Night Football and reruns of Gilligan's Island," she said.

"Hey, don't knock Gilligan's Island. When I was a kid I had a crush on Mary Ann."

He made one or two more cuts, then picked up a pair of needle nose clippers. As gently as before he began to trim a few additional spots, some so small that they were barely even visible.

The tree was only a foot tall and half that again wide, yet for Gideon, there was as much satisfaction caring for it as would have come from looking after one of the ancient redwoods he had seen as a child in Northern California.

And then it was gone.

Gideon stared, unsure if he could trust what he had just seen. In place of the bonsai stood a crow, ink-black wings glistening in the light. The bird cocked its head and stared at Gideon for a moment, then seemed to lose interest in him and looked elsewhere.

"What in the hell!"

For a long moment, Gideon stared at the bird.

And then it too was gone.

The tree was back, exactly where it had been. Gideon's fingers brushed across it, half expecting the branches to be nothing more than light, air, and dreams, but the tree was as real as it had always been.

"If I didn't know better I'd say I had been taking some very good drugs," he said

"Hardly."

Standing at the door to Gideon's workroom was— *someone*

The stranger was a tall lanky figure wearing an ankle-length duster, black shirt, and knee-high boots. Gideon could not quite see his face, mixed in with shadow as it was, the features seemed indistinct. As if they were there one moment and gone the next.

"I hope you aren't going to lead off with something really dumb and predictable, like "Who are you?" the newcomer said.

"Didn't I see you on one of the professional wrestling shows last week?" Gideon said.

"That at least is original," the stranger laughed.

He began to walk slowly around the room. Every once in a while he would stop and stare at various small trees and plants. When he came to the bonsai that Gideon had been working on, with one finger he began to trace the outline of the tree.

At a look from the other man, Gideon passed him the clippers. Three times pieces of leaf came away as the stranger's hand moved across the tree. Gideon stared at the bonsai. It was a subtle, but distinct, difference. Gideon nodded in approval.

"I've come for you, Gideon," the stranger said.

"Oh please. You were the one who said something about being original. Let me guess, you're Death, it's my time and that's why you've come for me. Come on, be a little more original," said Gideon.

"Death?" A thin line of a smile crossed the other man's face. "I suppose you could say I am, from a certain point of view, but not for you."

Gideon sighed deeply as he picked up a plastic spray bottle. A few squirts left a fine wet mist hanging in the air.

"So, if not Death, what are you then?" Gideon asked.

"I, friend Gideon, am you,"

"Me?"

"Yes, or I should say I am what you could have become had one little tiny thing been different in your life."

Gideon felt a twisting deep in his gut. He didn't want to hear what the stranger had to say. But he also knew that there was no way he could keep from it.

"What do you mean?" Gideon asked

"Cast your mind back. Back more than two years to a certain night," he said.

Gideon did not have to struggle to find that memory. It was always with him, now for the most part shut away, but always waiting to step forward.

Gideon and Magda had been returning from a celebration of Magda's parents' twenty-fifth wedding anniversary. An overturned truck on the expressway and a blocked exit had sent them trying to find a different route home. Only, this had led to abandoned neighborhoods that were unfamiliar to either of them. Then, in the flare of the cars headlights, in one moment, as they turned a corner, the two of them had found fear.

Against a wall, washed with a year of dirt, fire, and hatred, were two figures. Hauled high above a crowd of others they were spread-eagled, tied naked, amidst an arcane gang design, blood dripping from wrists, hands, and faces.

"I think we'd better leave," Magda said.

Leave they had. Gideon had jammed the accelerator of the cherry red '68 Mustang to the floor, throwing the car into a bootlegger's spinning turn that sent them roaring off in the opposite direction.

Neither spoke. For a moment he released one hand from the wheel and touched her. The smile she gave him was backed by a look of fear that cut deeply. Behind them, he could hear the roars of trucks and motorcycles as the Wild Ride gave chase.

*We're not going to make it*, Gideon thought with a certainty he hated.

That was when a man dashed into the glare of the Mustang's headlights. For a fleeting moment it occurred to Gideon that somehow, they had gotten in front of him.

He jammed hard on the brakes, yanking the steering wheel to one side. That sent Magda slamming hard against the door. The headlights rolled across the street like a roving spotlight to stop at the entrance to an alley.

Without hesitation, Gideon aimed the mustang into that dark maw. This might be the way out or it might be their death warrant. He only knew that it was the way they had to go.

"You chose wisely. That was what happened," the stranger said. His fingers brushed Gideon's forehead with the gentleness of a feather. "This is what could have happened."

Images rolled through Gideon's mind. Cold sweat rolled down his forehead. Memories that at first were familiar changed into things alien and terrifying. Instead of finding the alley, The Wild Ride had surrounded them. Magda was raped, beaten, and killed. He castrated, tortured, and dead. Gideon had to grab onto the edge of the work table to keep on his feet, the strength seeming to flow out of him in an instant.

"What are you?" Gideon demanded. "That's not what happened! "

"I know," the stranger said softly. "I know. It's what could have happened. Had it, you would have lain in a hidden grave, with Magda, for a year and a day. But you could not rest, not knowing what they had done to Magda. You will come back, as me, to avenge what happened by destroying those who killed you."

"That's not the way it happened."

"I know," the stranger continued. "I am what you could have become. I have always been. I always will be. Call me a god or a demon. I am vengeance, justice, the balance of scales."

"Then it was you, that night, in my headlights," said Gideon.

The stranger smiled. "I suppose you could say that. Know then Gideon, that I need you this night, to help spare another from the fate that was almost yours and your lady's."

The stranger extended his hand. Gideon didn't hesitate in taking it.

The fog had rolled in near midnight, a thick blanket, cut by the yellow light from Gideon's motorcycle's headlamps.

As he had slipped the worn leather jacket on, and the pair of World War One style goggles, Gideon had stared at the single window where a small light burned next to the bed. He knew that Magda was deep in studying the script for the commercial she would be shooting in the morning.

She hadn't heard him slip quietly out the side door and into the garage. With luck, he would be back before she even knew he was gone.

The stranger had said that he should just ride, that Gideon would know where he was going. So he rode. Vague shapes came and went in the fog, sounds drifted to him over the roar of the bike's engine. Every now and again he noticed a crow gliding in the air near him.

The neon sign was broken. Only the letters **B CK CAT BA** were lit. The wall outside featured a painting of a black cat swiping at a mouse with its paw.

This seemed as good a place as any to stop. Right now, a cold or even semi-cold beer would taste very good.

The bar was old. It smelled of smoke and beer. There were a dozen or so men at the far end of the room, dressed in the black and red vests that marked them as a small-time local gang, The Horde.

He walked up to the bar and dropped two dollar bills on it. A large mug with beer replaced them in a moment. Meanwhile, a tiny speaker began to play a song that Gideon wasn't familiar with.

A half dozen notes into the song the silver dance globe that hung above the stage. began to turn. Some of the silver plates that covered it were missing or broken, but it still produced a credible light that played over the room.

From behind a curtained doorway just to the side of the stage came a girl. She was thin, with short mousy blonde hair. She wore a two-piece dance outfit that had less cloth in it than most thong bikinis. Her face was masked in a pair of mirrored wraparound sunglasses.

The girl began to dance. At least she made some effort to match her movements to the music, though she didn't succeed often. A few of the patrons watched her, the rest were more in their drinks and the pool game that was going on.

"So, who is she?" Gideon asked when the bartender came round to see if he wanted another beer.

It was a question the man had heard many times. He grinned a sly knowing grin. "Oh, you interested in our little Bambi?"

"Bambi? Geez, nobody's really named Bambi."

"She is. That's cause everyone wants to Thumper," the man laughed, amused at his joke.

Gideon considered saying something but thought the better of it.

Any further comments by either Gideon or the bartender were cut short when two of the gang members began to disagree about a scratch pool ball. Only, they were disagreeing rather loudly and in each other's faces. Their disagreement escalated from loud voices to thrown punches in a matter of minutes.

At the same time, one of the men sitting around the stage made a grab for Bambi. Given the nature of the bar, this was something the girl was used to and she slid right out of his grasp. Unfortunately, while trying to stay on her feet she kicked a large pitcher of beer into the lap of one of the other men sitting around the stage.

"You bitch!" he yelled. He grabbed at her ankle. Since she was already off balance this was enough to send Bambi slamming hard into the floor.

Gideon was halfway across the room before he realized what his goal was. He had to shove several people out of the way as he went. The girl was on her side screaming as several of the other men made grabs at her. One managed to get her bra in his hand and ripped it free. He whirled the captured garment around his head like a prize.

By the time Gideon reached the stage Bambi had gotten to her feet. She was standing in a crouch, staring around her like a predatory animal ready to leap.

"Asshole," she screeched at him. "Touch me and I'll cut your balls off and feed them to you."

"Nice to meet you too. Shut up! This is no place to talk. Is there a way out of here that doesn't lead through this bunch of idiots?" he asked the girl.

Bambi hesitated, then pointed toward the door she had entered through. "There, it goes to the dressing rooms and a side door into the alley."

"Then what are we waiting here for?"

She led him through the curtain into a short hallway lit by a half-failing neon bulb. The dressing room was filled with cartons of empty beer bottles. One side held several small makeup tables and a clothes rack. A pair of jeans and a tee shirt hung at one end. The other was filled with several bikini dancing outfits, boas, and other props.

Bambi was reaching for her pants when the sound of a gunshot echoed from the main part of the bar.

"This is getting nasty pretty fast. Let's go," said Gideon. He grabbed her shoulder and headed them both toward the door.

"Hey, what about my stuff!"

Gideon ignored her and guided the two of them out into the alley. The sounds of sirens were growing closer and closer. There was also a small crowd of people who had gathered along the street to see what was happening.

*I guess everyone needs some nightly entertainment*, Gideon thought.

He pulled Bambi in the direction of where his bike was parked. She resisted, looking at the bike and him. "Hey, I'm not getting on that thing with you!"

"Fine! Suit yourself. But, off-hand, I would say that in about five minutes or less this place is going to be swarming with cops, not to mention assorted gang-bangers and friends. I have the feeling that you really don't want to run into any of them. Especially not dressed the way you are."

Inside he had guessed her at maximum of twenty-two years old. Now, looking at her dressed in the bottom half of a thong bikini and an earring, he doubted if Bambi was more than sixteen or seventeen.

Gideon headed for the bike. "I can drop you anywhere you want."

Without a word, Bambi followed him, then slid onto the bike behind him; her arms around his waist.

"Just don't try anything," she warned.

"Yes, dear," Gideon said.

*Don't worry*, he thought as he gunned the engine to life, *right now fucking you is the last thing on my mind.*

The crow sat on a phone wire above the fray and watched the whole scene.

Gideon fished into his jacket pocket for a crumpled cigarette pack. There were two that weren't crushed beyond any hope of smoking. Until tonight he hadn't felt the need for over six months.

The taste of both cigarettes flowed deeply into his lungs, a rough, uneven feeling, but welcome nonetheless. He passed one of them to the girl.

They had ridden for a half hour in silence, doubling and tripling back, crossing their route more than once. Finally stopping in an alley not more than four blocks from the Black Cat.

"So where do you want to go now, Bambi? By the way, what is your real name, anyway?"

She stood holding the cigarette, her arm covering her bare breasts, shivering in the cold and looking irritated at Gideon's question. "It really is Bambi. I can't help it if my mother was scared by a Walt Disney film when she was small."

"I guess it beats being named Ariel or Esmerelda."

Her only reaction was a dirty look in Gideon's direction. "It's pretty obvious there is no way I can go back to the club. I guess I'm out of a job. My purse and clothes are still back there, but they aren't any great loss. I only had about six dollars and the clothes were Goodwill specials. I suppose I could go over to Angela's place. She's out of town for a couple of weeks. I can stay there until I figure out what to do."

"Then that's where we'll go," Gideon said.

He looked down, running a critical eye over his motorcycle. There didn't seem to be any damage, beyond a long thin scratch on the gas tank. He wasn't even sure how fresh the mark was.

A sudden sharp pain smashed into Gideon's back. A second followed a few seconds later and sent him to his knees, struggling to keep from passing out. He twisted to one side, trying to find his attacker.

Only instead of a cop or one of the gang members, it was Bambi standing there, a long rusty pipe in her hands. She was glaring at him, daring him to move.

"Sorry," she said. "Trust is not something that I'm really long on right now. What little I had for you, I've run out of. The only one I can trust right now is me."

A moment later she had tossed the pipe to one side and climbed onto the back of Gideon's motorcycle. The last sight he had of her was vanishing down the street, sirens and shots echoing in the distance.

Gideon managed to pull himself upright, even though the world continued to whirl around him. Warm blood seeped across his forehead. He tried to wipe it away with one hand. By the time he had managed a step or two, it had slowed down considerably.

Gideon began to wonder if this were all real or some bizarre dream.

Whether it was real or not, Gideon knew he had to keep moving. The smell of garbage and gas fumes was turning his stomach. If he stopped he would be puking his guts out in a matter of seconds. There were a few other people on the sidewalk. Most looked at him and then went back to their own lives. Some stepped away to the other side of the street.

Gideon found himself in the middle of a spray of approaching headlights, the screech of wheels on wet concrete echoing around him as a car raced toward him. He tried to shield his eyes and see where the car

...sharp pain...sent him to his knees...

was but could barely make out shapes and forms in the glare.

Almost at the last minute, the approaching car cut hard to the left. Gideon could feel the rush of air as it passed within a half dozen steps of himself. Then it roared off into the dark of an alleyway.

"This way."

Gideon felt someone grab hold of his arm, pulling him quickly from the sidewalk and into the shadows. "Just wait and watch," said the now familiar voice of the man who had brought Gideon to this place.

Not more than a minute later the street was filled with a pack of motorcycles and trucks. Gideon looked at them, at the stranger next to him, and the quickly empty street.

The stranger's black lips were not smiling, but they seemed to have a satisfied look on his face. The crow was sitting on the man's shoulder.

"Would you mind telling me something?" Gideon asked, "Like what in the fucking hell is going on?"

"Everything and nothing."

"Yeah, right. I want a straightforward answer and you give me one of those Zen things, like what is the sound of one hand clapping or something like that. Thanks a lot."

"You're welcome."

"Is there even the remotest chance that I might be able to get a straight answer out of you?"

"Why don't you ask yourself the questions instead?" said the stranger.

"Me?" Then it came to him. The vague memory of the car that had almost hit him, a hint of red and familiar lines; the certainty that it also had a dented left fender and a slight alignment problem that pulled it to the right.

"So it wasn't you that we almost hit?"

"I don't recall ever saying that it was." the other man said. "Remember, I told you that I needed your help. Help that would keep someone from dying. I never said who that someone was."

Gideon looked away. A few steps from him, growing in the dirt at his feet was a single white rose. He reached down and touched it. The petals were moist from the night air, soft as silk, smooth, vulnerable, and yet strong as it held onto life.

"Magda," he whispered.

"Yes," Her voice was the same low whisper it had been the first night they had met. Gideon turned and found her standing at the door to his workshop. A vision in lace, shadow, and light. The slightest hint of a smile invited him to her lips.

From the ledge outside the stranger watched, a single tear rolling down his face, as the stranger smiled and then became one with the blackbird that sat next to him.

## The End

# GHOST

After three years of war, I thought I had seen everything.

The last thing that you expect to see on a hot afternoon in Richmond is a ghost. And certainly not one standing in the front door of the capital building of the Confederacy.

Well, I saw one.

I tied up my horse at a hitching post on the southeast corner of the building, in an area away from the main door. I had arrived a quarter hour early for my appointment with General Morgan Girard, my commanding officer. A soldier, obviously on guard duty, approached me, his rifle carried low in his left hand.

"Excuse me, sir. This area is restricted to Army officers only."

"As well it should be," I said. "Which is exactly why I'm leaving my horse here."

"Sir," he said. "It's for <u>Army</u> officers only. The civilian areas are around the corner." He put a special bit of emphasis on the word Army.

Because of the nature of my work, I've been more often out of uniform than in one. There are places where a uniform would stick out as much as Abraham Lincoln walking the streets of Richmond.

I held my identification where he could see it.

"Sir, I'm afraid I can't.....read," he said.

"That's all right, son. I'm Captain Adam Thorne, Military Intelligence."

He eyed me for a moment, then snapped to attention, his rifle sliding down to rest at his side in the proper manner.

"Sir, sorry for bothering you. I've been ordered to stop any civilians from leaving their animals here."

"Not a problem. You just keep on doing your duty. I wish more of our people were as adamant as you.

"Do you have a match, private?" I said as I pulled a cheroot from my inside coat pocket. He passed a Lucifer match to me. I had just dragged it along the bottom of my boot when I saw the ghost.

She was standing at the top of the stairway, looking off into the distance. Jenny, a vision in blue, her long red hair hung loosely on her shoulders, the parasol in one hand, to protect her from the sun.

"Jenny?" I muttered, unsure of even the sound of my own voice. Not that I expected her to hear me.

"Captain? Are you all right, sir?"

63

The guard was looking at me with that uncertainty that a lot of enlisted men seem to have when dealing with officers. Before I could do or say anything, pain shot through the tips of my fingers. I realized that the match had burned down and was attempting to steal a few seconds more of life by using my flesh as its home. I dropped the burning ember and stamped on it with my foot.

"Captain?"

"I'm all right. My mind was elsewhere." When I looked back, she was gone. If she had ever been there in the first place.

The memory of the headstone bearing her name was as fresh as the first time I had seen it three years before. No, it had to have been my imagination, it couldn't have been Jenny.

Yet...

"Right on time. Not that I would expect anything less than that from you, Thorne."

Brigadier General Morgan Girard stood up from behind his desk. He was not physically a big man, standing barely five foot eight inches tall, yet he always seemed to fill whatever room he occupied.

Girard had recruited me within a week of when the war for independence had begun. As a graduate of West Point, I had expected to serve our new country in the regular army. Instead, I found my talents being put to use in other ways. Our office was attached to the Secret Service, but they preferred not to talk too loudly about the connection.

"It's always good to see you, sir," I said. "I was sorry to hear about Mrs. Girard. I know her death must have taken a great toll on you."

"Thank you, Adam. These last few months have been very hard. But thankfully, I've had the boys, George and Derrick. They've been a source of great strength for me," he said.

"I've been told it was her heart?"

"Yes, I came into the bedroom one morning and found her. She had slipped away in the night. She just lay there, peacefully. I sat with her for an hour, before I kissed her cold blue lips and found the strength to summon the rest of the house," he said.

There were very few things, outside of his job, that I had seen Girard care passionately about. His wife, Allison, had been one, his two sons the others.

"Well, I'm not the only one to have lost loved ones in this war, so enough about me. Let's talk about what you're going to be doing next. I think you'll find it not nearly as big of a problem as that matter in New Orleans," he said.

That would be a relief. I preferred not to dwell on the New Orleans matter any more than necessary. There were, at times, things a soldier had to do in service for his country. You didn't have to like them, but they had to be done. New Orleans had been one of them.

"I'm putting you in charge of security for Lord Anthony Case-Jones."

"I take it this fellow isn't your average traveler on a Grand Tour over here instead of in Europe."

"Far from it. He's a special representative from Prince Albert, sent here to prepare recommendations on the question of diplomatic recognition."

Girard didn't have to explain the significance of that move. Diplomatic recognition would be a godsend for this country. It could bring us aid and allies, which we desperately needed. I had concluded a few months earlier that, shy of a major miracle, there was no way that we could win this war.

This might be that miracle.

"You'll meet his lordship tonight. He's staying with an old family friend of mine, James Collins," said Girard.

"So how does his lordship feel about having a shadow?"

"It doesn't really matter what he wants or doesn't want. He will be protected," said Girard. "I'll send a carriage for you tonight at eight. We dine at nine."

I knew when I had been dismissed.

"Captain Thorne! Captain Thorne!"

I was just fastening the last button on my waistcoat when someone started pounding on my hotel room door. My watch indicated half past six.

"Captain Thorne! Captain Thorne!"

"A moment," I answered. After slipping on my jacket I picked up a small pistol from the table. Just because someone knew my name and where to find me didn't mean that they had my best interests at heart. There are certain things that you have to do to stay alive. Better to do them and not need them than to lay bleeding and regretful minutes later.

"Yes?" I said, standing to one side of the door.

"Captain Thorne. General Girard sent me. My name is Cole Masterson," he said.

Cole Masterson turned out to be a lanky man in his thirties. He had an odd accent; one that I couldn't place.

"I wasn't expecting anyone until eight."

"I understand, sir. However, something has happened and the general wants you to come to the Collins house as soon as possible. He sent me with a carriage and orders to bring you there straight away."

"Can you tell me what happened?"

"No, sir. The general said he would brief you upon your arrival," said Masterson.

That sounded like him. I dropped the pistol into my coat pocket, picked up my hat, and motioned Masterson to follow me.

The Collins family home was an elegant three-story affair, built at the turn of the century on the south edge of Richmond. Several rooms on the first floor were so brightly lit that they fairly glowed in the fading July sunlight.

We were met by a man in his fifties, balding with a fringe of iron-gray hair, whom I presumed to be the family butler. He was accompanied by a young nigger boy who took charge of the carriage without a word.

"If you gentlemen would come with me. You're expected," said the butler.

I didn't know too much about the Collins family. The great-grandfather had immigrated to the United States just after the first war for independence. They had extensive mine, manufacturing, and farm holdings.

Girard was waiting for us in the entrance hall. He wore his usual grim expression, an unlit cigar in his mouth.

"Good evening, sir," I said.

"Ah, you made good time, Thorne. Masterson, I need you to take this to the Naval Office." He handed an envelope to Masterson, who promptly saluted and left without a word.

"Well, Thorne, I had hoped that this evening would be a pleasant interlude for the both of us. So much for those hopes," said Girard.

He motioned for me to follow him through a pair of double doors into what proved to be the library. It was a big room with floor-to-ceiling bookcases and a fireplace at one end. Two oil lamps were the only sources of light.

The general gestured toward a wing chair in one corner. Someone sat there, a man in his late forties with heavy sideburns and a dark tropical tan. His eyes were milky gray stones sunk deep into his face. Only, now that I looked at him, it wasn't his face that caught my attention. What looked like a long red sash ran across the front of his jacket, up over his shirt, and onto a deep gash in his neck.

"Do I take it that this might happen to be the gentlemen whom you wanted me to keep alive? Lord Anthony Case-Jones?"

"Indeed."

Well, so much for that assignment. I glanced around the room and in a dim mirror on the far side of the room, I saw the ghost again. Just for a moment, peering out from a book-lined alcove on the other side of the room. Except that this time it was wearing the black dress and white-collared uniform of a maid. It was Jenny! She was gone just as quickly as she had been the first time I saw her.

"Well, I don't know what recommendations his lordship had in mind, but I would say that someone did not approve of it," I said.

"Then you agree with me that this is very likely the work of Yankee agents?" said Girard.

"Possibly," I said. "Who all is in the house?"

"Just Collins, his lordship's traveling secretary named Rodney, and us. The rest of the Collins family has been living on one of his plantations near Florida for the past six or seven months. There are several hired servants, the butler who you met, a cook along with a couple of general handyman types," said Girard.

"What about slaves?"

"Amazingly, none. The handymen are niggers, but they've both been manumitted. I honestly hope that we find out it is a personal thing, rather than a political one. That will make it far easier to explain," muttered Girard. "But whatever the reason, I want answers as soon as possible."

"If you would get everyone in the living room, I think we can begin there," I said. "I want to have a closer look at a few things about his lordship, here. Shall we say in fifteen minutes or so?"

"Agreed," said Girard.

After he left, I gingerly slid my hands into the dead man's pockets. There was little there of interest: a handful of coins, a pencil, and several peanut shells. My manipulations caused him to slump to one side. That was when I noticed an inch or so of chain sticking clear of his shirt collar. It held a medallion of some sort. I thought at first it was one of those religious ones, but when I drew it free I could see a single letter engraved on each side.

"Don't you think it's about time that you came out?" I said.

There was no response, certainly not from his lordship. But he wasn't who I had been speaking to.

"I saw you in the mirror. I'm going to presume you've been listening and watching since then," I said.

To my left, I heard the slightest sound of metal creaking and hinges at work. Out of the corner of my eye, I caught sight of one of the bookcases swinging back into place.

"Can I get you a drink?" said the ghost. She looked every inch the proper ladies' maid. Her red hair had been wound beneath a white mob cap. At first glance, it would have been hard to recognize her, but this close there was no mistaking my sister, Jenny.

"Yes. Scotch."

She poured me two fingers of amber liquid from a bottle on a table near the fireplace. Then poured herself a twin of my offering.

"I hope you don't mind drinking with the hired help," she said.

"As if you were really the hired help," I said. "I imagine the only reason that you are employed on these premises is because you wanted to be."

"A girl has to earn a living," she said defensively.

"Are you saying that Davis Walker doesn't pay his spies well enough?"

I've always enjoyed being able to pull a rabbit out of my hat and surprise my sister. The astonished look on Jenny's face was enough to prove that I had not lost my skill.

"Not bad, little brother, not bad at all."

Major General Davis Walker was Girard's opposite number on the Northern side. I had encountered one of his men in Cuba six months before. We had gone to West Point together and considered ourselves friends still, despite political differences. Besides, our particular assignments at that time did not conflict, so we spent the evening drinking and reminiscing. It was somewhere past the second bottle of rum that he mentioned to me that Jenny had gone to work for Walker.

"Looks like there are two Thornes in the spy business now," he said.

"So, do you like working for the enemy," I said.

"Adam, I don't consider what I do as working for the enemy. I'm working for the country that we were both born in. But let's not get started on any political discussions. I had enough of them with Father. How is he, by the way?"

"Still as hardheaded and stubborn as ever. You know that he considers you to be dead. He even went so far as to erect a headstone for you in the family plot."

I'd been there the day that he had had it set in place. I suspect he would have held a formal funeral service for her, but my mother, and the local parson, had said no to that idea.

He and Jenny had disagreed on things for most of my life: slavery, politics; the proper way to respect one's parents. Their shouting matches were legendary in our family. It had been her falling in love with Nathan Jackson and wanting to marry him that had driven our father and her to the breaking point. It had stormed the night the two of them drove off together, four years ago. That had been the night my father had announced that as far as he, and the family, were concerned, his daughter Jennifer was dead.

So I suppose, from my father's point of view, I was talking with a ghost.

"You heard about Nathan?" she asked.

"Yes, a botched bank robbery and he was in the wrong place at the wrong time. Was that what drove you to work for Walker?"

"Among other things," she said quietly.

"You responsible for this?" I gestured at his lordship.

"Hardly. We learned he was coming and I was sent to keep an eye on him. A dead envoy will not help the United States' relationship with Great Britain. It might even be enough to drive them into recognizing you.

"Besides, it is my understanding that he was going to file a report saying that the English should stay neutral in the whole matter. Something to the effect of letting us settle our own internal matters," she said.

"This is hardly the way you normally investigate a murder," said Girard. "However, you all must realize this is not a normal murder. Otherwise, we would have summoned the local police at once."

Girard was pacing back and forth in front of the leather couch that took up most of the main living room of the Collins house. Our host, James Collins, was a man in his mid-fifties but seemed older. He stood near the large bay window that dominated the room. Seated near the door was Alexander Rodney, the late Lord Case-Jones' traveling secretary.

"Sir, why are you wasting your time here," said Rodney. "It's obvious that a Yankee agent murdered his lordship. You should be pursuing him. The fiend is no doubt halfway to Washington by now."

I didn't like Rodney's tone and his presumption.

"We are pursuing all avenues of investigation, Mr. Rodney. Not just in this house, but elsewhere, as well," I said. "Do you have a particular reason to believe that the North even knows that you are in this country?"

The secretary's face burned red with anger. "Of course they know we're in this country! I have no doubt that detailed reports of our every move are making their way to Abraham Lincoln's desk in each morning's mail!

"Are you aware, sir, of the delicacy of our trip here? There are members of the government who do not want to grant the Confederacy diplomatic recognition. They want us to formally ally with the United States against you."

"The general has seen fit to brief me on your mission. I only wish I had been brought into the matter sooner. Perhaps we could have prevented this murder," I said.

"I doubt that," said Rodney.

"Mr. Collins, where were you and Mr. Rodney earlier this evening?" I asked.

"Business kept me away from the house for most of today. I had barely returned home when Morgan discovered his lordship's body. I last saw him this morning at breakfast. In fact, that's also the last place I saw Mr. Rodney," said Collins.

"Don't go trying to accuse me, sir. It was Northern assassins!" said Rodney. "In the last fifteen years, I've traveled to many countries with his lordship. But this is the most vile one I think I have ever encountered!

"General, the stories you told us of this country, were enough to frighten any sane man. But all they did was make his lordship want to come here all the more."

"You had met Case-Jones, before, General?" I asked. It was a fact that he had not mentioned.

"Yes, Mrs. Girard and I spent a year in Europe and England before the war. I believe we met him at the Burton estate in Sussex."

"Enough of this!" snapped Rodney. "You must stop gibbering like old women and find the killers. They are getting farther away with each passing minute!"

"Oh, I think not."

"Really? Would you care to explain, Thorne?" said Girard.

"Actually, gentlemen, I know who killed his lordship. I have only one more matter to confirm before settling this entire matter," I said.

The sitting room and bedroom that had been assigned to Case-Jones were midway down the hall on the house's third floor. It wasn't locked; there was no need. So I let myself in. If the whole thing were the work of Yankee assassins, then no doubt they were, as Rodney seemed so convinced, long gone.

Everything in the room was as neat and orderly as if the maids had just finished cleaning it. I opened the closet and found each of Case-Jones' suits perfectly arranged. Three pairs of boots, which I suspected were shined to within an inch of their lives, sat on the floor.

I was about to inspect one when something struck me hard across the back of the head. The blow didn't knock me out, but I had to grab onto the door frame to keep on my feet. Whomever my attacker was followed with a swift kick that connected to my hip and almost sent me down.

Somewhere in that process, I realized that I still had one of Case-Jones' boots in my hand. I threw it at my opponent, missing, of course, but that bought me time enough to get steady on my feet and face him.

Without really thinking, I threw myself against him, sending both of us tumbling down. What I presumed to be a knife went clattering to the wooden floor. My pistol was in an inside coat pocket and caught between the two of us, essentially unreachable.

"I'd suggest that you boys call this whole thing off right now!"

Jenny! She was standing with a gun of her own in one hand. The expression on her face was as cold and unfeeling as any I had ever seen.

"Are you all right, Captain Thorne?" she asked. Better to not acknowledge each other.

"Aye, and very grateful to you."

I looked down at the familiar face of my opponent. Morgan Girard.

"You're insane, Thorne," said Girard.

I'd had the butler summon the two nigger handymen who were now standing on either side of Girard. He hadn't wanted to come back to the living room, but the barrel of the gun I had taken from Jenny and held in the small of his back provided a powerful argument in favor of doing what he was told.

Jenny had excused herself, claiming to feel close to fainting now that it was all over. Officially, she had been passing by the room, heard the scuffling, and went in to investigate. Actually, I had left her hidden in the hallway, waiting to see who might come along.

"See here, Captain Thorne, I hope that you know what you're doing," said Collins. "I've known Morgan Girard since we were both small children. I cannot conceive of the idea that he is a killer."

"Then perhaps you had best learn," I said.

"So, what is it you're claiming? Is he a Yankee spy and killer?" asked Rodney.

"Killer, yes. But I doubt he is a Yankee spy. I have no doubt of his loyalty to the Confederacy. He just wanted us to think that a Yankee spy was behind the murder. It would keep people from realizing that it was a matter of jealousy, revenge, and, more than likely double murder."

"Double murder?" said Rodney and Collins at the same time." Who?"

"Yes, I'm fairly certain that in addition to murdering Lord Case-Jones, Girard also killed his wife Allison," I said.

"Thorne, you have become a monster. You know Allison died of a weak heart," said Girard.

"Indeed, I attended her funeral," said Collins.

"But do we know that? We have only his word and the word of a doctor who no doubt made no close examination. This morning Girard told me about discovering Allison's body. He mentioned that her lips were cold and blue. It strikes me now that that may well have indicated death by either poison or suffocation," I explained.

"But why? And why kill Case-Jones?" asked Collins.

I took out the medallion that I had removed from his lordship's neck and held it out where the others could see the disk. On one side was a stylized A and on the other an M. But the M had been obliterated.

"This is significant?" asked Rodney.

"It is, indeed," answered Collins.

"You know?" I said.

"I was there when Morgan had those made. They were his wedding present to Allison, one for her, one for him." Collins's face had grown still, showing no emotion.

I didn't have to look to see that Girard still wore his, under his shirt. I had seen it on several occasions before.

"I would suspect that during their sojourn in England, Allison Girard and Case-Jones began an affair. That was no doubt when she gave him the medallion. At some point, Girard found out about it but opted to do nothing. Perhaps he felt having an ocean between the two lovers was enough. That was until he heard that his lordship was being sent here as a special envoy. That was when he made up his mind to have his revenge, on them both," I said.

I had wondered why he had gotten me involved in the whole matter. The only reason I could conceive of was that he thought my loyalty to him would let him conceal anything too incriminating.

"This is a fine tale you've spun, Thorne," Girard said. "But it is nothing but pure fantasy. It's obvious to me that you've gone over the edge, the pressure of the war. I've seen it in others who've worked for me. Trust me, son, I'll see that you get the best medical treatment."

"Morgan, shut up," said Collins. "He's right. You told me yourself that you knew Allison had had an affair. You know the hidden passages and panels in this house almost as well as I do. We spent many hours prowling them when we were children. So I would say that the best thing to do right now is to keep quiet."

I expected Girard to do something. But not what he did. Instead of making a grab for a weapon and trying to escape, he reached into his coat pocket and brought out a small enamel snuff box. With a slow dignified, manner he administered several pinches to himself.

I don't know exactly what was in it, but the reaction came a few seconds after he set the box down. He went stiff for a moment and then his head slumped forward on his chest. I didn't bother to check; if he wasn't dead, then it was only a matter of a few minutes. Perhaps this was better than the gallows or a firing squad.

Still, the whole matter left a foul taste in my mouth. I didn't say a word to Collins or Rodney as I excused myself, went out into the hallway, and lit a cheroot.

A few minutes later Jenny came up beside me. "Not the most pleasant circumstances for reunions, little brother," she said.

"No, no it wasn't."

Jenny reached over and plucked the cheroot out of my hand. She lifted it to her lips and took a long puff from it, then blew the smoke out in slow series of rings

"I know you looked up to Girard. He was a good man who went wrong, somehow," she said.

"I think we all have that potential, little one."

"You know, you're a pain, but I definitely like having you around. Be careful, and don't you go wrong," she said as she passed the cheroot back to me.

"I'll try." That I was speaking to empty air didn't surprise me. My big sister is good at what she does.

"Is there a problem, sir?" The butler came from the direction of the kitchen, looking at me rather oddly.

"No, no, nothing that won't eventually right itself," I said. "I was just standing here thinking."

"Very good, sir, although I did think I heard you speaking to someone a moment ago," he said.

"Actually, I was. One of the maids, the one with red hair," I said.

"Red hair? You must be mistaken, sir, we have no maid with red hair. Besides, both of them have been working in the kitchen for some time," he said. I could see the slightest sparkle in his eye.

"Perhaps I was mistaken. Who knows, maybe I was chatting with a ghost," I said.

"Quite possible, sir," he said.

## The End

# GRAILS

If he could have had anything just at that moment, anything in the world, Jared Santee would have wanted a cigarette followed by a drink, several of them. Oh, they were available, an all-night convenience store for the former and any bar could help with the latter.

Only Jared knew that he wouldn't. That would be a sign that she had won since he hadn't had a drink in six months or a cigarette in more than two years.

Instead, he just stood in the doorway of the abandoned building and stared out at the street. His thoughts— and they were many and varied, for he couldn't find the comfort of forgetting, right now— raced from one to another. Always though, they came back, back, to one image, Laura; her laugh, the feel of her hand in his, the provocative promise her smile held as they walked along the beach, and just the sheer joy of having her in his life brought forth in him.

But, that was gone now.

The sudden screeching of tires as an old pick-up came too quickly around the corner brought Jared back to the present. As he watched the truck head off toward the docks he caught himself almost expecting to see another one coming after it in hot pursuit.

"You've been watching too many old movies," he said and suppressed a tired chuckle.

Jared looked around. He vaguely recognized the street, somewhere in the old city district. It was mostly warehouses, with a few decrepit apartment buildings mixed in. What few businesses there were had been long since locked up behind the protection of rolling steel shades.

"Jared, Jared, Jared," he muttered. "You're getting far too morose for your own good."

The green glow of his watch read, 2:15 a.m... Four hours since he had walked out of his condo on the west side, not three minutes after he had walked into it. Instead of the greeting he had expected, the kind that had awaited him since the day a year ago when Laura had moved in, he found only a single sheet of typed paper waiting for him; pinned to the purple hippo they had used to leave messages for each other.

*I'm leaving. Don't try to find me. I don't love you. I don't want to see you again.*

"It's not like you're the first man to ever get a Dear John letter," he said to the night. The words did little to do away with the deep gnawing ache in his gut.

There was a single word painted on the wall near Jared; repeated over and over again. Each one a different color, each one a different style, all repeating the same word.

WHY?

"Why not?" he muttered and drew a deep breath, letting it go slowly as if it were cigarette smoke. This was not the moment for deeply universal philosophical questions. Jared had enough of his own, and right then they all boiled down to the samequestion the unknown graffiti artist had posed.

WHY?

Jared had no idea how far he'd walked, or for how long, when he heard the crashing sounds coming out of the alley. Standing just where he could see him Jared spotted a small man; perhaps four feet tall at the most, he wore a black duster-like jacket that swept the ground. There was something almost feral in the way he held himself. In his right hand, he held what for anyone else might have been called a long dagger, for him it was a sword. A sword that had blood along its surface.

"Yeah?" he demanded when he saw Jared.

"Sorry to bother you."

"Well?" the little man demanded again.

"I heard the disturbance and thought that I'd see if I could be of any kind of help," Jared told him.

"Nope, though I appreciate the offer, I got everything under control for now." The small man gestured further back into the alley.

Two bodies lay a dozen steps away. He had the feeling he knew where the blood had come from. They were dead. Nothing living could be forced into the unnatural positions Jared saw. One of them looked like it had lizard-like skin. The other seemed to have odd protuberances on its back. Wings?

"It may be none of my business, but you've got me curious about something," asked Jared.

"What?" asked the little man.

"Them," he gestured toward the bodies, not entirely sure that he wanted to know the answer. "Who are or should I say were they?"

"A couple of pains in the ass," grinned the little man. "Low-level enforcers for a local entrepreneur who claims I owe him money because of the outcome of some recent sporting engagements."

"Are you saying they work for a bookie?" Okay, at least this had a touch

"A couple of pains in the ass."

of something familiar.

"If you must use such a coarse term," said the little man. "Yes, a fellow by the name of Blaylock."

The little man took a long silk scarf out of his sleeve and began to carefully clean his weapon. When that was done both weapon and scarf vanished beneath his coast.

"Well, I guess there's nothing that I can do," said Jared. "I'll be on my way."

Before Jared could turn away the little man looked up and down the street and began to stroke his chin. "You know, now that I think about it, if you wouldn't mind, I could use a bit of a favor. And no, before you ask, it doesn't involve lending me money."

"That's a relief. "

"Well, I was just on my way to deliver a package." From another place under the jacket, he pulled a small package. It was wrapped in brown paper and sealed with clear plastic tape. "Don't worry it isn't drugs. I was taking this to an antique dealer over on Garabaldi Street. Realistically speaking, I think I may need to disappear for a while, at least until I can straighten things up with those fellows' employer. Problem is I did promise to deliver this package and it needs to get there ASAP."

"So what's in it?"

"I told you not to worry about that; it isn't anything illegal. Plus I think I can make it worth your while to do it."

Three coins hit the ground at Jared's feet. Heavy and yellow. Krugerrands was his first thought. But when he saw the profile of Miss Liberty on one side and a double-headed eagle on the other he knew that wasn't what they were. Each one was in as pristine condition as the day it had been stuck and bore the date 1883.

"I don't know..." he began but realized that he was alone.

"Damn," muttered Jared. He picked up the package and read the address. Grails, 127 Garabaldi Avenue.

"Grails?"

WHY?
As he walked, Jared kept remembering the graffiti-painted wall and its multiple depictions of that question. Once he had gotten himself oriented

Jared realized that he wasn't that far from Garabaldi Street. Only a matter of a few blocks to the west and then another dozen or so to the south.

The further he went the more rundown looking the area became. No bright history now decaying away here, it felt like a place that had started out decaying and forgotten.

"M'boy, what have you done got yourself into now?" Jared's common sense said that the best thing to do right now was to just set the package down on the ground, leave it and the coins, and go back home to his condo.

Yeah, that would have been the sensible thing to do. Certainly a lot more sense than walking down a deserted street in some god-forsaken section of town, doing a favor for some escapee from a bad road show company of The Hobbit.

Maybe that was why he didn't do it, mused Jared because there were times when you just didn't want to do the sensible thing. He had no doubt that Laura would be saying that this was yet another one of his damn fool ideas and he was getting himself deeper into trouble with every step he took. That had been the thesis for many of their arguments over the past months.

He spotted Grails from a half block away. At first glance, there was nothing particularly outstanding about the store, except for its very existence in this neighborhood. It looked like any one of the hundreds of small businesses that Jared had seen over the years, a small storefront, family-owned operation that was more than likely just getting by.

The most extraordinary thing about the place was that it appeared to be open at this time of night. A convenience store or a gas station was one thing, but a place called Grails?

A good part of the store's window was taken up with intricately detailed lettering that formed the store name. He could see display cases just inside, but not what was in them. In the lower right-hand corner of the window was a small plastic sign that read "Open, Please Come In."

Jared touched the door handles. The metal was cold. When he turned it and pushed the door, the hinges groaned loudly, announcing his entrance...

"Hello?" he said.

No answer.

Given the neighborhood, he had been expecting a junk shop or perhaps a Pawn Shop where local thieves could fence their latest acquisitions. This was neither. Banks of neon bulbs hung close to the ceiling and illuminated the place as brightly as if it were daytime.

Several counters and wall shelves displayed a variety of items. There were swords, Indian masks, reproductions of paintings, watches of various kinds, even electronic gear, everything from Gameboys to computers, some so ancient a pile of punch cards and vacuum tubes lay next to them.

"Welcome to Grails. Can I help you?"

The voice was just another one of the things that Jared could add to the list of things that had surprised him since he had gotten off the plane from Baltimore. Standing next to him was a woman with short brown hair dressed in black jeans and wearing a cut-off Mozart tee shirt that left her midriff bare.

"Yes, good evening," Jared answered, feeling awkward as he heard those simple words coming out of his mouth. "I'm sorry to be bothering you this late. Although I'm more than a bit surprised to find you even still open at this time of the night.

"We're open when we need to be," she said, her voice touched with a 'don't make foolish comments' tone.

"Okay, that's cool. Look, I......"

That was when the side door came flying open. A human tornado, in the form of a tall thin woman with short blonde hair and glasses perched on the end of her nose, came rolling through it spitting piss and vinegar with every step.

"You!" The target of her ire was not Jared, considering he had never laid eyes on her before.

The young woman shook her head, a sad smile on her face, "Another satisfied customer," she whispered and turned to the new arrival. "Is there a problem, Ms. Lansdale?"

"A problem! A problem, she asks! Yes, there's a problem! That damn broach that you sold me is the problem! You said it was just what I needed to add that little bit of something to my new outfit and blow away the producers on the new series! It was supposed to cinch my being cast!"

"No, Ms. Lansdale, I didn't say anything about it assuring your getting the part. I just thought it would complement your outfit," said the brunette.

"All that producer did was proposition me! It made me so mad I dumped a platter of lasagna on his head."

"I'm sorry about that, but I never made any promises."

"You bitch! I told you what I wanted! Grails is supposed to give me that!" The Lansdale woman grabbed the other girl by the shoulders, clipping the edge of a display case. Both of them went tumbling to the floor.

Jared watched them for a minute. Then he grabbed the Lansdale woman by the shoulders, mainly because she was on top, and hauled her onto her feet. Trying to hold onto her was a struggle; she kept twisting and turning with every step as he forced her toward the front of the store.

"I think you better go somewhere and cool off, lady," he said forcing her out the door. "Come back later, when I'm not around!"

"Since you got rid of her, the least you can do is offer me a hand up," said the other woman.

"Oh, sorry." Her grip was tight and strong. Jared had a feeling that had it come to fisticuffs she would have come out the winner.

She straightened her shirt, brushing her hair back into place. "I never promised her that the broach would be what she wanted. I just said it was what she needed, and in the long run, I think it was. I'm pretty sure, in a couple of days, she'll get a call from a casting director who saw her little performance with the producer, and who wants her to audition for a sitcom."

"I don't understand."

"It doesn't matter, Mr.....I'm sorry I didn't get your name."

"Santee, Jared Santee."

"My name is Tanith Zachary. Now, understand that I do appreciate your stepping in to help. But there wasn't any need; we do occasionally get unhappy customers. It wasn't anything new."

"All right," nodded Jared. "I wasn't planning on coming here tonight, anyway. In fact, until a little while ago I didn't even know Grails existed."

"Really? That happens sometimes, Mr. Santee. So, welcome to Grails. How can I help you tonight?"

"It's more like I'm helping someone else out," Jared offered the package to her. "I ran into this little guy a few blocks from here. He asked me to deliver this to you."

Tanith's face went pale when she saw the package. "Who gave you this?" she demanded. "Is he still alive?"

"Hold on! Yes, he's still alive; at least he was about fifteen or twenty minutes ago. I never got his name, a little guy in a longish coat."

She ran her eyes up and down Jared. "About four feet tall, most of it solid attitude?"

"The poster boy for attitude."

"Rupert!" she muttered under her breath. "There are moments I wonder why I don't kick your butt from her toe San Francisco!"

"Look, he was okay. Some...things had jumped him and...."

She held up her hand. "Wait, you need to be telling this to my father."

"Okay, by me, I guess. Did you say the little guy's name is Rupert?"

"Yeah. Got a problem with that?"

From her tone, Jared had the feeling that Rupert wasn't the only one who had a large dose of attitude. "No! Shall we go talk to your father?"

It wasn't long until Jared was completely lost.

Tanith led him to the back of the store and down a narrow hallway. Their route soon passed through room after room, down some staircases, up others, through more hallways than he thought he had ever seen in any building; more than he was sure should have been in the old building that housed Grails.

Some of the rooms were storage areas, with narrow walkways between huge crates, the light so dim that he could barely see Tanith a few steps ahead of him.

Other rooms held the weirdest assortment of items that Jared had ever seen; from a gargoyle statue with a clock in its belly to costumed dummies wearing outfits that would have been contemporary during Prohibition; in one he saw an ornate coach and was certain that horses were whinnying in the far corner.

In the center of yet another warehouse-sized room, filled to the brim with still more packing crates, was a big mahogany desk and file cabinets; a laptop computer sat in the center of a large blotter, right next to an old-style Royal manual typewriter.

Sitting behind the desk was a man, his red hair streaked with odd gray highlights. He didn't seem to notice their arrival, as he was reading a comic book and had a pair of headphones wrapped around his ears.

"Dad," Tanith called out. When he didn't respond she stepped up next to his chair and pulled the headphones off.

"Oh, hello dear," the man said nonchalantly. "Is he your date for the evening?"

"Hardly," she snapped. Jared could feel the sting in that one word and didn't particularly like it.

"Sir," he said to Tanith's father. "My name is Jared Santee. I'm not really sure just what is going on here. I was asked to do someone a favor by delivering a package to your store. Just as soon as your daughter saw it she got highly agitated and said we had to come talk to you."

"Well, this is unusual." He extended his hand to Jared. "Forgive me, Mr.

Santee, my manners are lacking sometimes. My name is Nathan Zachary. You've already met my daughter. Let me welcome you to Grails. As you might imagine we operate a rather unusual store."

"I'll say."

"Dad, we really don't have time to give him the ten-cent tour. Look at that." She gestured at the package.

Zachary pursed his lips as he held it to the light. "Not good, not good at all," he said. "Is Rupert alive?"

"As I tried to tell you, daughter, as of a few minutes before I walked into your store, this Rupert, was very much alive. He was looking more than a little disheveled, but very much alive." Jared was getting a little tired of repeating this litany.

"Disheveled? How so?"

"Yes, apparently he had a run-in with a couple of guys who worked for some bookie, by the name of Blaylock

"That doesn't surprise me, Rupert and his gambling is nothing new," nodded Zachary. "Did Rupert give you anything else besides this package?"

Jared fished the coins out of his pocket.

"Oh, lord," said Tanith. "Rupert turning loose of money?! If he's done that then he's scared, really scared."

"Knowing Rupert he's probably into this bookie for a lot of money. He's probably been trying to draw to inside straits," said Zachary.

"Where is this Rupert getting mint condition Double Eagle's," asked Jared. "Aside from the metal's value do you understand how much each of those coins is worth just as a collector's item?"

"Quite a bit," nodded Zachary. "Let's just say that Rupert has access to those coins and a lot more like them. Of course, getting him to turn loose of any is a major production; on the other hand, he goes through paper money like its water."

"Dad, I think this is his way of saying he knows he's in big trouble and sending for help."

"I have to agree. I think this is his way of calling for help," a spasm of coughing ripped through Zachary. "Forgive me, it's a combination of asthma and malaria that acts up on me every now and then. So I'm afraid I'm not going to be in any shape to do anything about Rupert. Of course, there have been times when I would say that he wasn't worth going to the trouble of saving."

"Dad, he's family," Tanith said. "Leave it to me. Nice to have met you, Mr. Santee, hopefully, you can find your way to Grails again sometime."

She was gone before Jared could say anything. Her father just shook his head and sat back down in his chair.

"She is as stubborn as her mother."

"Excuse me, what in the name of all creation is going on here? What is this place? Who are you people?" asked Jared.

"It's funny you should use that particular phrase, Mr. Santee...all creation. You might say it fits Grails. This store is, shall we say, a central point for things, things that people have lost and want back. People come here because they need to find their way here.....and my daughter and I try to help them find what they are seeking. Sometimes they don't even know what they're looking for."

"This is sounding a little too Twilight Zone for me. I suppose. Are you saying this is where all those socks that always disappear end up?"

"Sometimes," laughed Zachary. "Before you ask, I have no idea why it happens. It just does. People come here looking for something, it might be things major or minor but it is important to them. They will find what they need at Grails, it might not be what they want, but it will be what they need. Tanith and I, along with my late wife, have just tried to help the people who come here."

"And Rupert is one of those people?"

"He came in the door about twenty years ago and quite surprisingly kept finding his way back. We get few repeat customers. I think he sort of needed a family, that's what he got with us." As he spoke Zachary opened the package up and removed a leather-covered jewelry box. Inside was a silver necklace that held a green wire-wrapped stone that reflected the light into a rainbow. "Rupert helped us raise Tanith, even suggested her name. I guess you could say he's kind of like her godfather," he began coughing again. "Gads, I hate it when my own body is acting against me. Look, I'm afraid that Tanith may need help. She's as stubborn as her mother and would never admit that she needed help, even to herself. I know I have no right to ask, but I'm going to anyway. Is there any chance you might be willing to go with her?"

For no reason that Jared understood, he nodded. "Why not? If I get myself killed, it will fit with the rest of the things that have happened to me tonight."

"Take a wrong turn on your way out?" asked Tanith.

Jared shook his head.

Her father had been quite detailed in the directions and he had no trouble finding the dressing room. Tanith had exchanged her tee shirt for a sweatshirt and was putting on a vest of what looked like Kevlar armor when he walked in.

WHY? That was a damn good question. Jared didn't have an answer and he didn't think that there was going to be one anytime soon.

"I'm exactly where I need to be," he said.

"Look, I don't have a whole lot of time and I sure don't want to have to be babysitting you tonight. If Rupert has gotten himself involved with who I think he might have then it's going to get a mite rough out there."

"You mean that bookie, Blaylock."

"Exactly. You stand a pretty good chance of getting yourself made very dead tonight. So why don't you take off," she suggested.

When Jared just stood there looking at her, Tanith shrugged. "Okay, it's no skin off my nose!" She went over to a small cabinet and began to go through several of the drawers, pulling out several items that she slipped into her pockets. "Look in that closet over to your left. I think you'll find some armor that will fit you."

Indeed he did. The armor wasn't all that heavy, not like conventional Kevlar, but it had a sturdy feel to it and helped to bolster his confidence. This whole thing was crazy, definitely down the rabbit hole and falling deeper.

"Are we going to be needing guns?"

Tanith shrugged and gestured at a set of drawers. "If you feel the need," she said. "Third and fourth drawers over on the left. Ammo should be to the back."

There were half a dozen pistols of various sorts, from revolvers to automatics. Jared picked a Glock automatic. The clip fit snugly into the gun's butt; two others went into his pocket.

Tanith handed a sheathed Bowie knife, a twin of the one hanging from her belt. "In case we need to work quietly."

"Am I correct in assuming that you have some kind of idea where Rupert may have gone to ground? He did say that he would be needing to disappear."

Tanith laughed. "Rupert has his own definition of things. His idea of making himself scarce means going to a different bar than the one he normally hangs out at or getting his meals at a Chinese joint rather than an Italian place."

As he followed her, Jared found himself with the oddest feeling that they had forgotten something, a nagging sensation that wouldn't let go, he just couldn't think of what it was.

"Having second thoughts?" asked Tanith as they passed the desk where her father had been sitting. There was no sign of Nathan Zachary.

"Hold your horses for just a minute." The wrapping paper was exactly where the elder Zachary had left it, though it took a moment to spot the necklace. Only the thin silver chair was visible, hanging over the edge of a plastic police riot helmet.

Jared grabbed the necklace, the nagging feeling slipping away as his fingers wound through the chain.

"What are you waiting for?" asked Tanith.

"Nothing. I think we're ready now."

"How nice of you to say so."

"Look, if you want me to take you for a midnight stroll, just say so. Maybe next time we can leave the armor at home and I can bring you flowers."

"Shut up," Tanith whispered.

They had been on Rupert's trail for just over an hour, visiting a pool hall, an all-night diner, and a twenty-four-hour liquor store. But still no sign of him. As each one of them turned up empty Jared couldn't help but notice that Tanith was getting into a fouler and fouler mood.

"Tell me again why I came along?" he asked himself.

Finally, they came to Harridan Park built five years before, with the idea of the place being the centerpiece for the rejuvenation of this part of the city. Only it had been mired in bureaucratic bickering since the original contractors had gone bankrupt.

At night the only ones who were seen in the park were the homeless, gang bangers, and a few others who preferred that their business not take place in the light of day.

"There's just a chance he might be here. Says it reminds him of Ireland."

"Rupert is Irish?"

"He'd like to think he is."

Before Jared could say anything more he spotted Rupert. The little man was standing near a park bench, about fifty feet from them, busily rolling a cigarette. What looked like several predecessors lay on the ground, suggesting that Rupert had been there for some time.

"There he is! Let's grab him and get out of here."

"No, wait. I've got a bad feeling about this."

A man, dressed in a western shirt, jeans, and wearing a baseball cap stepped up beside Rupert and spoke. They were too far away to hear what was said, but the little man's face had gone pale when he realized he wasn't alone. The newcomer produced a lighter and held it close enough to light Rupert's cigarette.

"Well, well, well," said Tanith. "We may have had a bit of luck after all. When you said it was Blaylock who had laid off Rupert's bets, I thought it was the old man. Instead, it looks like we're dealing with junior, his number one son."

"Is that good?"

"Matter of opinion." She pulled a stone out from her pocket and pushed it into Jared's hand. "This will let you see things the way they really are."

Jared did as he was told. Rupert appeared the same, but there had been some changes in the other one. His hands were now covered with fur, as was his face which had also taken on a distinct wolf-like appearance.

"Are we talking werewolf bookies?" he said.

"Lycanthropes is the proper term. But werewolves will do. Young Mr. Blaylock doesn't like to work alone. Look back in the bushes," whispered Tanith.

Two other men were standing some distance back from Blaylock. Even at this distance, he could see their wolf-like features.

"So, do we call a dog catcher?"

"Hardly." Tanith looped her arm around Jared's waist. "Put your hand on my ass and try to act like we're the only people in the world. With a little bit of luck, we might live another ten minutes. Just be ready to do something when I say so."

"I think I can handle that," he whispered. Right then, it occurred to Jared that he hadn't thought of Laura for some time and that didn't bother him in the least. The pain was still there, deep in his gut, but it was something that he would deal with later. He suddenly knew that he could.

Whether Rupert recognized them Jared didn't know. The little man had dropped his cigarette and started rolling another one. This time around his hands were so shaky that he could barely get the makings out of his pocket.

Jared could see, out of the corner of his eye, Blaylock watching them as they passed. When his attention shifted back to Rupert, that was enough. Tanith launched herself at him, driving her shoulder hard into his chest. The collision was enough to send Blaylock stumbling backward. Before he could do anything Tanith kicked him hard in the knee. That was him on the ground.

Jared leveled his gun at the other two. "You've got to be joking," one of them said.

"Silver bullets. At this distance, I can't miss and it'll rip whatever I hit to shreds."

"One of us could take you."

"Maybe, maybe not, but I'd sure as hell get the other one. Which one of you wants to volunteer for that job?"

Tanith had her arm around Blaylock's neck, the bowie knife against his throat.

"Now, listen up fur face. This blade is solid silver, blessed by three different popes, two chief rabbis, a voodoo priest, and a whole bunch of other people who would just love to see me use it to skin you alive!"

"You bitch! I'll rip your guts out and pan-fry them," Blaylock screamed. "Do you know who I am? Even if you manage to get away, I can promise you that you won't live long enough to see the sunrise."

Tanith pulled the edge along Blaylock's throat. A tiny trickle of blood followed it. "Trust me on this one, dog breath. I'll live a lot longer than you if you don't cooperate."

"I'll grind you...."

"Offhand, junior, I would say that she's got you where she wants you. I'd try negotiating with her if I were you."

A gray-haired man dressed in an elegantly cut silk suit, holding a black wooden cane, with a silver cobra head in one hand, stood next to the park bench.

Jared squeezed on the stone that Tanith had given him. When he looked at the man, he saw the image of the biggest, meanest-looking wolf that he had ever imagined, overlaying that of the human. This one made the others look like ninety-eight-pound weaklings.

"Father! She's using some sort of witchcraft to get an unfair advantage. I can handle this whole thing," growled the younger lycanthrope.

"I really wonder why I brought you into the business. Maybe I should have financed that blue grass band you wanted to form. Oh well, hindsight is twenty-twenty." The older Blaylock pointed his cane at Rupert. "I have a breakfast appointment with the mayor. So let's see what we can do about bringing this whole thing to a peaceful conclusion. Rupert here is hardly worth a fight."

"I barely know him," said Jared. "And I agree with you."

"Hey," yelled Rupert. "I just asked you a favor and you insult me!"

"Shut up Rupert," said Tanith.

"Look I'm just defining my reputation. I'm the one who is being insulted..."

"Shut up Rupert." Tanith, Jared, and the elder Blaylock all said at once.

"How much does he owe you?" asked Tanith.

From inside his jacket, the older man produced a small account book. "Let's see, rounding off a few numbers, it comes to just over fifty thousand. Rupert, did you really start placing bets on girls' volleyball?"

"Hey, I had some insider information."

"But you lost."

"A run of bad luck. It can happen to anyone."

"Shut up Rupert," said Tanith. "How about we trade you; Rupert's IOUs for your son."

"I suppose you realize that knowing this little reprobate, he'll be back making bets by this time tomorrow."

"That's then, this is now. So will you do it?" asked Tanith.

"All right. It's a deal. Maybe this will teach my pup to be a bit more selective on whose bets he takes. But I will require something else, a token payment in lieu of what Rupert owes me."

"Such as?"

Jared acted without really thinking, pulling the necklace he'd taken from Zachery's desk out of his pocket. The stone was glittering even in the dim light of the park. This felt like the right thing to do. "Will this do?"

Blaylock walked closer, looked at it for a moment, and nodded. The stone vanished into his hand with a single movement.

"Come, junior, you two follow me. Oh, Tanith, would you please give my best regards to your father? Tell him I'll see him Thursday."

The Blaylocks were gone, as soundlessly as they had come. Jared slipped his gun into his belt and turned to Tanith. "Your father knows that guy? What's Thursday got to do with it?"

"That's when they play pinochle."

The eastern horizon had begun to glow a ruddy red, though stars still held sway in the rest of the sky. Jared had the feeling that in daylight this part of town would only look worse than it did at night.

After they had left the park neither he nor Tanith said anything. Rupert, on the other hand, had many things to say, on several subjects. Most of them boiled down to the fact that he was one of the nicest guys in the world, extremely misunderstood and the world did not appreciate his genius. After a block or two, Jared had pretty well tuned him out.

When Tanith finally spoke, he heard her quite clearly.

"Why?"

"Why what?"

"Okay, smart ass," she said. "I'll rephrase the question. Why did you do it? Go with me, I mean, and end up risking your neck to save Rupert."

Jared had been asking himself that, as well. Oh, there were any number of pithy one-liners he could toss off, such as "Why not" or "It seemed like the thing to do at the time," but those weren't right.

"You went because you've known him all your life. What did you tell your father, 'he's family?' I guess I went because he needed help and I needed to do something for someone else. That's about the only answer I can give you."

"It'll do."

"Well I, for one, am glad that you knew to pack silver bullets," Rupert said.

"Yeah, that's something else I was wondering," said Tanith. "How did you know about the silver bullets? You didn't know anything about the lycanthropes until we got to the park."

"Oh, that," laughed Jared. "Who said I had silver bullets in my gun?"

"You did," said Rupert. "I heard you tell those two pug uglies."

"I lied."

The strands of one of Beethoven's early symphonies drifted out of speakers set back from either side of Nathan Zachary's big mahogany desk. He leaned back in his chair, eyes closed, and savored the music. It had been one of Elaine's favorites; on their first wedding anniversary, he'd taken her to a concert that featured it.

"God, I miss you so very, very much, sweetheart," he whispered.

"Are you getting sentimental again?"

"Shut up, Rupert."

The little man sat in a Papasan chair just to one side of Nathan's desk. When Nathan finally opened his eyes he noticed that Rupert had picked up the wine bottle and was shaking his head as he looked at the label.

"What's the matter?" asked Zachary.

"Really, Nathan? The '63? You've got a lot better vintages in your cellar than this. I should know, I helped you stock it."

"Stop being such a wine snob; it's a perfectly good wine. Just pour us a drink and answer my question," he told the little man.

Rupert poured several inches of wine into two glasses and passed one across the desk. "You had a question?"

"Yes. Don't play smartass on me. Are you sure?"

"Of course I'm sure," said Rupert, smiling. "Jared said he said he 'felt' that he 'needed' to be there to rescue me and that he 'needed' to take the necklace along. Sounds just like what you've been wanting."

Nathan hoped that the little man was right. The proper person "knew" what a particular visitor to Grails 'needed'. Not what they wanted but what they needed. That was the key. The key to Grails. Nathan had always described it as an itch at the back of his neck; one that he couldn't scratch until he found what was 'needed."

"I've been wanting to retire now that Tanith is old enough, but she needs someone to help her run this place," said Nathan. "So I think I'm going to offer Mr. Jared Santee a job here. I don't know much about his background, but I suspect this place might fit him to a tee.

"Tanith is going to love this. The last time I saw them they were fighting like cats and dogs," said Rupert.

Nathan smiled and took a swallow of wine. "Sort of reminds me of when Elaine and I were first married. Who knows, this may not be what my dear daughter wants, right now, but I have a feeling it is exactly what she needs," he laughed.

## The End

# CORNERS
# IN DARK

From the moment I saw The Charon Company's Number Six oil rig I knew something was wrong with it, and that made it just perfect.

I had originally intended to come by helicopter. A twenty-minute ride as compared to an hour-and-a-half boat trip was a no-brainer. Mechanical problems with the chopper shot that plan down, so I went to plan B, the boat.

Boats are not one of my favorite ways to travel, but I didn't have a lot of choice in the matter. We were scheduled to start shooting the first episode of the season in just over three weeks and there were two other filming locations that I needed to visit in the next six days.

Two of my team members were already on the platform. They'd headed out here without me because my plane was late getting into the New Orleans airport. Of course, the fact that I was now following them into the Gulf of Mexico just as a storm was blowing up did not thrill me in the slightest.

Thankfully, I was able to hitch a ride on a regular supply boa. It visited a half dozen rigs, dropping off enough groceries and assorted spare parts so the people who worked on them could eat for another week and not feel too cut off from the world.

Unfortunately, the regular route the supply boat took ended up making Charon Number Six the last stop before heading back to shore. So it was after nightfall when I watched the oil rig slowly grow in my view, like a dark hand coming out of the water. It was majorly impressive.

Some of the bigger oil well rigs have been described as floating cities. Charon Number 6 wasn't anywhere near that big, just a hundred feet long with three levels, along with the actual drilling tower.

"This will definitely work for the opening," I said.

My show, it's called _In Dark Corners,_ by the way, is what is popularly called a reality show. We go to places where people claim to have experienced hauntings or seen some kind of legendary animal. Then we film our investigation and hopefully find something. The latter rarely happens, but our ratings are good enough to say we're reaching an audience.

"Opening?" asked Amy Barker, the boat captain, a no-nonsense woman in her thirties. She wasn't bad looking, in a don't-mess-with-me-or-I-will-deck-you sort of way.

"On my show, we always start with an aerial view of wherever we're filming, a high altitude shot, and then zoom down to ground level," I said. "But this time I think it will work a lot better to come shooting along the water at sunset and let the rig just grow out of the water. I think I'm going to end up steering some business your way."

"Okay, Hollywood, whatever you say, as long as your check clears," she laughed.

"Do I get the feeling that you don't like my show? Or maybe you've just never watched it."

"You're right on the money there, Hollywood," she chuckled, a self-satisfied grin on her face. "I haven't watched it. You've got to own a TV to be able to watch anything."

"Unless you can take care of your business in a short time, with this weather we may be spending the night here," Amy said.

"Then I hope you brought your jammies," I said. "Because there's no way I can do what I need to do that quickly. So, I guess we're bunking here tonight."

"I sort of figured that," she chuckled, and pointed toward a heavy black backpack that lay on the deck near her feet. "I'll come up top in a bit. I need to make sure everything is secure."

A scratchy voice came from just out of sight at the top of the stairs, "Well, it's about time you got here and started doing some work."

If I didn't hear J. W. "Jake" Connelly welcoming me with those exact words, I would worry that something bad was going to happen. It's not that I'm superstitious, but when he didn't greet me like that we'd had equipment malfunctions twice and once had to hightail it out of an African country just ahead of a coup-de-tat.

"If you think I'm going to say I'm glad to be here with you, then you've been hitting the moonshine a bit too much, and not sharing," I laughed.

At five-four and a hundred and forty pounds soaking wet, Jake certainly doesn't look like one of the best location scouts and line producers in the business, but he was exactly that. I was just happy to have him on my crew for the past two seasons. He says he agreed to come and work with me because I beat him at poker. Personally, I think he lost deliberately just so he could thumb his nose at some studio execs.

He led me along a metal walkway that you could look down through and see the water forty feet below. Knowing that just an inch or two of steel was standing between you and it could easily leave a queasy feeling in someone's stomach.

The main operations center was a decent-sized room. A desk at the center of it was illuminated by three long neon tubes. The only real light in the room was the bank of neon over the table that Nadia had commandeered. There were a couple of solitary bulbs hanging over the main door, but they looked like the sort of thing you would see in a low-budget horror movie, the ones that flicker and then go out at just the wrong time.

I could hear the sound of a small generator that I presumed Jake had brought with him.

Nadia Forester is one of my researchers and a co-investigator. She's the ultimate cynic and is always looking for a mundane explanation for the things we're investigating. She's able to squeeze into places that would give a non-claustrophobe claustrophobia. The standing joke among the crew is if she can get her blonde ponytail in somewhere, then she can get the rest of her body through the opening.

"Hi, Russ," she said looking up. "I was wondering if you would make it out today with that storm moving in. The coffee is over there."

I've heard stories of rock stars who demand that bowls of only blue or purple M&M's or a certain kind of Italian mineral water be in their dressing room. I don't know if those are true, but I know I'm nowhere near that bad. With me it's just coffee, but not some highly special brand that comes only from a tiny little coffee shop on west 35th Street in New York, just regular everyday coffee that you can get in any grocery store.

I found the small portable coffee maker and poured myself a cup. Given that the temperature felt like it had dropped at least ten degrees since I had gotten on the boat, even though the liquid tasted awful, I enjoyed every drop.

"Before you even say a word about the coffee, just remember, you're the one who keeps saying there's no room in the budget for a portable espresso machine," said Jake.

"Yeah, yeah," I muttered. "So what have we got?"

Looking around the room, I still couldn't escape the feeling that there was something off about this place; maybe it was the darkness and the idea that there should be people and noise, and all we had was the wind, the

He led me along a metal walkway...

waves, and the darkness. It just didn't feel right.

"Russ, this has got to be one of the stranger ones that we've come across," said Jake.

"Aren't they all? That's what makes good television."

"Yeah, but this one is different," said Nadia. "The Charon Company is not one of the major players in the gulf oil business, but it does decent for a medium-sized company. Their other platforms have been turning a profit, but not this one. In the last five months they've had two complete crews of twenty-five men, all experienced oil patch workers, quit. Out of those fifty, twelve have committed suicide, five disappeared and eight have been committed to lunatic asylums."

"I believe the proper term is 'mental health facility,'" corrected Jake.

"Don't you dare go all PC on us," Nadia snapped. "Some of these guys, who seemed perfectly normal before they came here, went totally fruit loops. The rig manager's logbooks and reports talk about his men having frighteningly vivid nightmares, some of the men claiming that they heard chanting in the middle of the night coming from the platform and out in the water. Altogether, it makes for some bizarre reading; take a look."

Apparently, the rig manager had found one of his men, who committed suicide by hanging himself off one of the highest beams. Before offing himself, the man had carved a symbol into his chest with the rough edge of a screwdriver. It looked like some kind of runic letter, crossed with a hieroglyph of some kind. I know something about runes. I have a degree in drama, but I also have one in archeology. This didn't look like any runic alphabet I had ever seen.

"We have so got to include this," I said. "Is there any kind of translation available?"

"Not from anybody connected to the oil company. They claim it was just part of the ravings of a, now what did they say, 'poor sick individual who managed to slip past the mental health screening system'," Jake replied with a snort.

"So, do *we* have any idea what it means?"

"Well, I sent a picture of the drawing and a photo of the original to a friend of mine who works at the Bibloteqhue National de France. He got back to me wanting to know what kind of crap I was getting myself into," Nadia said.

This to me said he thought that she was on to something. I also didn't bother to ask where she might have gotten what was probably either crime scene or autopsy photographs of the actual rune. I learned a long time ago, with Nadia you don't ask too many questions. It wasn't that she wouldn't answer them; it was more that you might not want to know the answers. Besides, it also lessened any legal liability.

"So, could he identify it?"

"Yep, he said it represented a very old mythological god, a proto-Egyptian thing, with about two dozen different names, the sort of critter that likes to snack on the sanity of us mere mortals." I had the vague memory of having heard something like this on one of the other paranormal shows the network ran; okay, I admit it I try to keep up with the competition.

"All that sounds like any one of a dozen Hollywood producers I've worked for. So what else did your boyfriend say about this guy?" asked Jake.

"He's not my boyfriend," she said. "He's married to my ex-wife. I gave her away at the wedding, one of the smartest moves I've ever made."

That was when the door to the operations center whipped open and Amy came dashing inside, followed by waves of rain.

"Jeez, if I'd known it was going to get this bad I would have charged you double for the ride," she managed to say between gasps of breath. Jake pulled a blanket from one of the chairs and wrapped it around Amy's shoulders.

"Guys, this is Amy Barker. I hitched a ride out with her on her boat. Looks like the four of us are going to be rooming together tonight since the weather seems to have taken a turn for the worse," I said.

"Well, we've got our choice of a couple of cabins and a big bunk room. After that suicide the feds ordered this place closed down while they conducted an investigation of the whole thing. How you got permission to film here, I have no idea. After all that trouble with the Deep Water Horizon I would have thought they wanted to keep weird incidents quiet," said Jake.

"Just my charming personality, plus they claim the official investigation is done," I explained. Frankly, I figured they were going to try and cash in on the publicity of having a possibly haunted platform. As long as it helped the ratings of my show, I didn't care.

"Yeah, right," she muttered, wrapping her hands around the Styrofoam cup full of coffee she had poured herself, as much for the warmth as the liquid. "So, where's your buddy?"

The three of us looked at her. "What are you talking about?"

"That guy I saw on one of the upper walkways," she said, looking at the three of us like we were idiots. "Big tall black guy, dressed in a long coat which, with the way the wind is getting up, is probably a good idea. He had a creepy-looking expression on his face. I caught him staring at me, and it wasn't in any kind of a nice way. You do know who I'm talking about."

"Actually, the only people who are supposed to be here on the platform tonight are the three of us and you. We start filming in ten days and the oil company is going to bring a new crew of roughnecks in a week after we finish," I said.

"Wait a minute; are you saying you saw someone, besides us, watching you?" Jake asked.

"Is this guy deaf or something, Hollywood," she turned to me. "I really don't like having to repeat myself."

This was beginning to feel like an episode of our show.

"Let's go find our visitor," I suggested, heading for the door and grabbing a flashlight from the rack near the door.

"Amy, where did you see this guy?" I asked.

"He was up there." She pointed toward an overhanging walkway that led off toward the north side of the platform. Several cables and hoses hung off the safety railing, which the last crew hadn't bothered to properly store away.

Naturally, by the time we got up there, there was no one to be found. Of course, that didn't mean that our "friend" might not be standing within ten or fifteen feet. All the steel girders and hoses, along with the drilling equipment, were a maze to deal with during the daylight hours, so at night and in a storm, it made invisibility a real possibility.

"Jake, go up to the next level and see if there is anyone about. While you're at it, would you please be careful? We don't need you getting hurt, especially not now," I cautioned.

"Yeah, the paperwork that Russ would have to fill out would be a royal pain in the ass," chided Nadia. "Not that you wouldn't look cute hobbling about on a pair of crutches."

"Yeah, you would probably laugh your head off," said Jake.

"Jake, get your ass up there." The night vision goggles that we used on the show would have been helpful right now, but they, along with the rest of our equipment, were back in Los Angeles.

"I wish now we'd gone with the O K Corral investigation," Nadia lamented.

"We've got some objections coming from the Arizonian historical commission; think having TV people investigating the ghosts might be bad for business," I said.

"Hey, Hollywood, you guys into tag art?" asked Amy. She had lingered down on the main part of the platform when the three of us had come up here.

"Tag art?" Nadia echoed.

"Over here," she led us back down the stairs toward the far end of the platform. On one side of a small storage building that, even in the sea salt-heavy air, reeked heavily of oil and grease, was covered by a huge mural. It was hard to see details, but what had been painted there was a huge version of the scarred design that the roughneck had carved into his flesh.

Nadia reached up and gingerly touched a part of the design. "Ouch," she cried and jerked her hand away from it. "What the hell was that? It was like sticking my finger in an electric outlet."

"I always said that you had an electric personality, kiddo," I said.

"Trust me on this, find whoever it was who said you had a sense of humor and beat the living daylights out of them, asshole." Nadia began to flex her fingers as she massaged her hand trying to get the feeling back into it.

I was seriously beginning to wish that we had gone to Arizona. Even with that idiot historical commission hassling us, I would have felt more in control of things than I did now.

I looked down at the water forty feet below where we were standing. The surface was covered with white foam slapping against the sides of the rig's supports. For a moment I was almost certain that I saw something there in the water, man-shaped, and more than one of them, twisting and turning around the rig. Then whatever I saw was gone. I decided not to say anything, again feeling like anything I might say would sound more like something out of the show.

The wind had shifted, again. That was when, for just a moment, I could hear something. It was some sort of chanting; the sound had a distinct rhythm to it; making me remember the chanting at a voodoo ceremony when we had done an episode last year in northern Louisiana. I couldn't make out the words; nothing was completely clear, but I had a churning feeling in the pit of my stomach listening to them. Whatever they were, the words were gone almost before I could hear them. But they left a foul taste in the back of my mouth.

"I think we better get ourselves back inside, Russ," yelled Nadia. She kept nervously looking up toward the higher parts of the platform, scanning the area again and again.

"You're right," I agreed. "Where the hell is Jake?"

"Knowing him, he found some nice dry little cubbyhole up there, thinking to ride out the rain," Nadia offered. "He's probably sitting up there right now where he can see us and is laughing his head off that we're getting wet and he isn't."

That hardly seemed like the Jake I knew, but I wasn't going to say so. Right now, Nadia hardly seemed like the rational down-to-earth look-at—the-man-behind-the-curtain type. I thought that getting us inside and away from the elements wouldn't be that bad an idea, for all involved.

"The operations center, now," I directed; trying to sound as authoritative and confident as I could, even though I was pretty much confused, and if I had to admit it, more than a little scared.

I was pretty sure I caught a glimpse of someone moving on one of the walkways thirty or so feet above us. It had to be Jake; at least that was what I kept telling myself. Whomever it was wasn't running to try to get out of the rain, but rather moving at a slow steady walk as if ignoring the elements.

"You two get inside, where it's dry. I'll take a look around for Jake. He might need help getting back down here," I said.

Amy grabbed my shoulder, then pulled something from the small of her back and pressed it into my hands. I could tell from the feel that it was a gun.

"You be careful up there," she warned.

"Awww, you care," I chuckled.

"Maybe, but look at it this way, I'm just protecting my exclusive rights to bring you and your crew out here to film this place. Face it, in this economy I can use the money," she laughed and headed off with Nadia.

"Watch your ass, boss," Nadia added.

"You just make sure that there's some fresh coffee waiting for me," I yelled back.

I didn't do any fancy checking of the gun to make sure it was loaded; I trusted Amy on that. Besides, I know so little about guns that if it had been an automatic, I probably would have screwed things up quite badly. Thankfully, it was a revolver, so I slipped it into my belt.

I had some trouble making my way up the stairway; it felt like the wind was reaching tornado strength at times. I made it, but not without feeling like I had just completed one hell of a workout.

There was probably some fancy oil industry term for where I was, but I didn't know it and couldn't have cared less. There were two small shacks at opposite ends of the walkway, storage places for tools and other equipment,

I assumed. Those were the places to start, but the wind was getting so bad I had to start rethinking the whole search-for-Jake plan. So I turned around and headed back to the stairway.

That was when I practically tripped over him laying on the walkway. If I hadn't been keeping a good hold on the railing I would have been doing a swan dive over the side into the water.

"Jake," I yelled, but with the wind, I doubted that the sound of my voice carried over a few inches. He was cold, and wet and didn't move, which, given the circumstances, didn't seem all that out of the ordinary. But when I rolled him over to see what was the matter with him, I knew that Jake was no longer with us. The skin of his face was pulled tight around his head, so tight that I could see the clear outline of his skull. That hadn't been true only a handful of minutes ago when I had seen him head up here. He wasn't breathing, or at least it didn't look like it. I tried to find a pulse but couldn't. I had to face facts, trying to maneuver his hundred and forty pounds of dead weight in this weather was going to be damn near impossible and I had a gut feeling that it wouldn't do any good. So I pushed him up against the railing, pulled his jacket off him, which was not an easy task, then used it to lash him there.

By the time I made it back down to the main platform and the door of the operations center, not only were my clothes soaking wet, but I felt like I had swallowed half the Gulf of Mexico. The transition into a room where water and wind weren't slamming against me was almost a physical blow. I could feel it in my chest as I gasped for breath.

Even before my eyes had focused I knew something was wrong. I heard Nadia making some sort of muffled sound from off to my left. When I could see, I knew that things were horribly wrong.

Standing ramrod straight near Nadia's work table was a tall swarthy-looking man with a vaguely Egyptian appearance. His face was dark as leather, which set off the strange gold-flecked eyes that stared at me, utterly repellent yet mesmerizing all at the same time. A rat came running out across the table, colliding with an empty soda can that someone had left there earlier. The creature looked around as if seeing if anyone had noticed its action, just then noticing Nadia's struggles. The animal reared up on its hind legs and stared at her for a few seconds before vanishing into the darkness.

Nadia and Amy were behind him, against the wall. Not standing, but adhering to the surface, Amy was a foot or so above the floor. I could see the look of terror on both women's faces. Nadia didn't seem to want to stop struggling; it was as if she did, that would be surrendering the very soul of what she was.

"I…"

At that moment, the man, at least that's what I thought he was, changed. Where he stood there was a pillar of churning blackness, a man-sized opening into utter chaos. Long thin tendrils of smoke, or something, reached out, first to the two women, who screamed. I could feel that sound in my very depths. I wanted to run, but my legs wouldn't do anything. As one of those smoke things touched me I was flooded with images, a dozen running simultaneously in my head. I couldn't sort out anything from this cascade except the sure knowledge that this thing was real and for whatever reason, someone among the roughnecks had set it loose. It was a struggle to even think, but I knew as certainly as I knew anything that this "thing" wanted out, wanted to walk the earth and one of us was going to be the way.

Right then, all I wanted to do was to rip my own heart out to escape this thing that was pulling me in, making itself part of me and my part of it. A part of me kept hoping that I would wake up with one killer hangover and remember this as only a very bizarre nightmare.

The last thing I heard before the darkness took me was the sound of my own screaming.

"Russ, I'm glad you're here early, I've got the opening ready," said Carl, the show's chief editor, as I walked in the door of the editing booth.

I set the large Styrofoam cup of coffee I had in my left hand down on the edge of the CPU and took a seat next to Rick.

"So, what have you got for me? "I could smell something in the air, a vaguely burning stench. "Are you overloading one of these very expensive machines?" I asked with a grin.

"No, I punched the wrong time on the microwave and ended up burning the crap out of my frozen burrito."

"Figures. So, have you worked your magic for our opening sequence?"

"Your idea was terrific. It works great."

The screen in front of us lit up, first with a close-up shot of the water and then the prow of a boat shooting through it. Then the camera rose to the darkened horizon and you could see the oil rig seeming to grow out of the water. That still sent shivers down my spine.

"Welcome, friends, as we seek to find out what is hidden in the shadows, what we see just out of the corners of our eyes, and, most of all, what is right in front of us In The Dark Corners of reality."

The camera panned across the other members of my team and then settled on me for just a few beats; seconds later our show logo came up and the opening credits rolled.

"Nice job, Carl," I said.

"Thanks, boss. Your new team is pretty colorful, but I still miss Jake and Nadia," he said.

"I do too, Carl."

"By the way, I love that effect the new night vision goggles' light does to your eyes," he said, picking up a half-eaten piece of pizza from next to his keyboard.

"My eyes?"

"Yea, it makes them look like they have gold spots in them."

"Never noticed that. We can call it my new look," I grinned, looking at the tiny gold flecks in my eyes reflected in the monitor on the control panel.

## The End

# LINES IN THE SAND

The surf had been building up for nearly an hour. Uneven bits of white mixed in with blue reached further and further up the sand.

I had left Jack somewhere back up the beach. There had been this intense political discussion going on between a bunch of graduate students from UCLA. It was the sort of thing he could never walk away from.

For a long time, I just sat there in the cleft of two rocks and watched the ocean. It reminded me of a July afternoon, oh, so long ago, when George Barris and I had done a beach photo shoot. The wind, the sand; it had all just fitted together perfectly. I only wish we'd had time to do it again, the way George wanted.

A couple of seagulls were working their way along the shore, diving and lifting again on the wind, skimming down to the very edge of the water. I'd always felt a sort of kinship with them, so free, able to reach out so far, yet so tied to a specific set of circumstances.

"So, you're really going to try."

Leaning against the rocks was an all too familiar face. Bobby! He shook his head, absently pushing his hair back in a familiar gesture. I hadn't heard him come up, but that didn't surprise me in the least. I knew *why* he was here and I honestly don't know if I was happy or not by his making the effort to show up.

"No, I just like the beach. Are you here for another fight?" I asked. "I hope you at least made yourself useful and brought champagne with you?"

"We didn't always fight," Bobby said. "There were some good times, some very good times. Besides, you know champagne makes you giggle."

"So what's wrong with an occasional giggle?"

"You're really going to try?" He repeated.

"Of course I am. You knew that when you came." Just to the left of my foot, I noticed a sand crab scrambling toward the rocks. "Wouldn't you, if you were me?"

"I hoped I was wrong. You know all it's going to do is end up hurting, hurting very badly." His accent had come back, deeper and more distinctly New England than ever.

"Why not? It wouldn't be the first time I've been hurt," I said. "You've

104

tried. We all do. It's allowed." There were other things that I wanted to say to him right then, but I didn't.

"You're wrong there. I haven't tried, not that I haven't thought about it, but I still haven't," Bobby said. Maybe it was just his attitude; he always did have an ego bigger than his native Massachusetts. I knew that this was his way of admitting that he cared enough to try to stop me, without really admitting that he was doing it.

I turned and looked at the ocean again, listening to the waves, feeling them move more than actually seeing them. When I did eventually look back, Bobby was gone like he'd never even been there.

I don't know just how long I sat there, but the next thing I noticed was the last rays of the sun shrinking behind the horizon. The wind had grown colder, even though it was early summer. I hugged myself for warmth.

Finally, I got up and began to walk south along the beach, taking my shoes off as I went, letting the water and sand squish between my toes.

When I could hear the cars up on the highway, I knew that I wasn't all that far from the restaurant. It had been opened by some Major fresh out of the Army Air Corp who used his retirement pay to open it, hoping to cash in on the money that was supposed to abound in sunny California.

I spotted her sitting on a rock not too far from the water's edge. The tide was moving up close enough to occasionally touch her toes. The giggle told me a lot about her mood. She had a long stick and was drawing idly in the wet sand.

Dressed in a canary yellow blouse and tan slacks, her brown hair hanging loose around her shoulders, she seemed to have a sort of innocent optimism about her. No, that sounded too much like the sort of crap the studio publicity offices put out. The problem was, it was true, despite the pain, frustration, and desperation that I knew lurked beneath the surface.

I stopped a few feet away from her. She looked up and smiled, as she continued to draw. Finally, she stopped and stared at her creation.

"It needs...something," she said.

I looked down at it. "May I?" I asked, reaching for the stick.

I began to make a series of lines in the sand next to her drawing. I had no particular design in mind; I just drew what struck me at that moment. Gradually it came closer and closer to the first one, never quite touching hers, but seeming to merge, nonetheless.

"That's very good," she said. "Are you an artist?"

I hadn't been all that sure I could get her to talk to a complete stranger. But sometimes people will open up to a stranger, precisely because they are just that, a stranger.

"I wish. I just doodle here and there."

"Well, you're good. What's your name?"

I hesitated for only a moment, my throat dry. "Mar...Just call me Mary, everybody does."

"Nice to meet you, Mary. I'm Norma. Though I've been thinking of changing my name." It seemed funny hearing that name come from her, in a voice I knew so well.

"Then you must be an actress," I said.

"And what makes you think that?" she asked, cocking her head as she spoke.

"The only people who change their names here in California are either bank robbers or actors. Since I didn't see anyone who looked the least bit like you on **Mr. Hoover's Top Ten Most Wanted List**, that can only mean that you must be an actress."

Norma giggled, her face flushed slightly from the wind. "You're right," she said. "Or at least I'd like to be. I haven't had a whole lot of luck with auditions, yet, but I'm going to make it."

"You sound pretty confident in yourself."

"If I'm not, who will be?"

"Good. You're what, twenty? That would be just a wee bit early to start declaring yourself a failure and throwing in the towel." I told her.

Norma rose and walked a few steps. There weren't any tears, but that didn't mean that there shouldn't have been or that they weren't far away.

"The problem is, I am only twenty, and I do have my whole life in front of me. A whole life of failure if I don't fight things every step of the way. I've failed a lot of people, let them down, in those twenty years," Norma confessed without looking up. "My mom. My foster parents. My...husband. I'm scared I'm going to fail again if I don't work very, very hard at it. Sometimes I'm even too scared to try because I might fail, and that hurts..."

I picked up the words for her. "...so much that it cuts right through you until you feel like there's nothing else. Yeah, I've been there more than once myself, kiddo."

"What do you know about show business?"

I wrapped my fingers through each other and looked toward her. "I've been in more than my share of movies."

"Extra work is easy to get. I've never heard of you."

"It happens. I've been where you want to be, and sometimes the price just doesn't equal what you end up getting for it," I said, trying to inject as much "truth" into my words as possible. "If I were you and I could, I would take a long, hard look at things. Maybe it's not really worth it."

"Right! The only thing is, you've given up. I can see it in your eyes," Norma said. "What are you, thirty-five? By the time I'm your age I'm going to be on top of the world or dead. You may have given up, but not me. My big break is out there and I am going to find it."

"Did you ever think about what it might cost?" I asked, already knowing the answer to that one all too well.

Norma turned her head just slightly toward me. "What do you mean?"

"It's a lot of long, long hours, far too little sleep, no social life except, maybe, what the studio orchestrates for you. As for the directors and producers, forget them; they don't see you as a talented actress, just a walking, talking pair of tits that needs to be told where to stand, when to speak, and to stay out of trouble.

"And as for marriage, that's a joke. Tell the truth; how many Hollywood marriages do you know of that have lasted all that long and are still happy? Most of them are staying together because of pressure from the studio. And then there's kids; you and they would be virtual strangers if you're working a lot, no matter what kind of garbage the publicity department dreams up."

Norma drew a long breath, pursing her lips in and out for several minutes. "I know it won't be easy. You may not know it, but I've been modeling for the last couple of years. That was long and hard and it cost me my marriage and even more."

As I recalled, technically she was still married; it would be another month before the divorce was final.

"I understand."

"Besides, if I made a go of it, I don't believe those things you talk about will happen to me. I'll make it work and work right," Norma's voice had just the slightest tremor in it.

"So what does your date tonight think of your chances? "I asked. "There are an awful lot of other beautiful girls kicking at the studio gates."

"You know, it's funny. That's exactly the same thing that Jim, my ex-husband used to say. As for Bob, well, he thinks that I've got the makings of a star." She flipped her hair back, smiling, to emphasize the last word.

"So, is this Bob an actor as well? You know, it's not a good idea to date other actors. Though the publicity department really eats that sort of stuff up."

"No," she shook her head. "He's a writer, I practically tripped over him today at the studio," she smiled at the memory.

"From that tone, I'd say that you like him," I said, taking the wise older woman's position. "I get the feeling you like him a lot."

"I do. He's fun. He makes me feel special."

"That's important. Maybe the two of you would be better off just packing it up and going back to Ohio."

Norma picked up the stick and began to add lines to her sand design, each one cutting deeper and deeper into the sand. "You know him, don't you?" she said at last.

"Who?"

"Bob. Bob Slatzer. You know him and you want him for yourself. You must have followed us tonight." Her voice was full of venom. "If you don't know him, how did you know that he was from Ohio?"

Whoops. "I didn't follow you tonight. I'm not trying to break up your date. Norma, listen to me. Think about what you're doing. It's not going to be worth it. No matter what it seems like now."

For maybe a minute she just stared at me.

"Oh, yes, it will be! Whatever the price I pay. I think you're just a sad old has-been who wasn't willing to do what it takes," Norma turned toward me with fire flaring in her eyes. "Lady, someday I am going to be a star and nobody will remember you. You're nothing, that's all you ever have been or will be. Get out of my way or I will crush you."

That was when another voice intruded on the two of us. "Norma!" A couple of hundred yards up the beach I spotted a young man in slacks and short sleeve shirt. My heart was in my throat; it was Bob. Bob Slatzer. Oh, Bob, it was special with you, but it could have been even more special than it was.

"Norma!" he called again. Norma jammed the stick into the sand, directly into the heart of the drawing, turned, and headed toward Bob at a run.

I got out of sight before Bob got much closer. He had never mentioned seeing anyone else that night. Of course, given the circumstances, the memory of making love in the sand with surf echoing around us, I could understand why.

Once they were gone I walked back around to the rock. The tide had already begun to cover the lines in the sand. I watched for a long time as the waves moved further and further up, wiping a bit more each time.

Well, that was that. The thing is, it didn't surprise me in the least. I could have talked until I was blue in the face and it wouldn't have done any good. Norma Jean was as thick-headed and stubborn as I remembered her, as I still am.

Just around the point, I found Jack waiting for me. He smiled, kind of sadly, and we walked for a long time, his hand slipping into mine.

"I guess that Bobby was right," I admitted.

"My little brother can be a pain in the ass at times, but he's usually right."

"I didn't change a thing."

"Did you really expect to?" he asked softly.

"I don't know. I just felt like she deserved the chance to find some happiness and maybe find a way out of the hole that I dug myself into," I said.

"Are you saying you weren't happy?"

"No, I was happy, at times very happy." I wasn't even sure if I was telling the truth or just what I wanted to hear myself saying.

"You want to try again? There are some other places, further on in your life. After she's got a movie or two under her belt. Maybe before Joe's gone or Arthur leaves. Then you can give her just the right push, keep things from..." He didn't have to finish the sentence.

"I doubt it. Who knows, maybe I'm saving the world from my career as an interior decorator who finally dies at the age of 65 in 1995. How many times have you tried to change things?"

He rolled his eyes up, shaking his head. "More times than I can count. Or even want to think about. Everything from trying to convince myself to stay married to my first wife to not trying to run until '64. Hell, I even tried to talk myself into staying in the Navy."

"Aye, aye, Admiral Jack. Hey, that does have a pretty good ring to it."

"Watch it, woman. I demand more respect than that from you; after all, I am the President."

"Were." I reminded him. "Besides, you were just a common politician. I, on the other hand, am a movie star."

"Don't get impudent, Norma Jean."

I think that was the first time he had ever called me anything but Marilyn. I squeezed his hand tighter and we walked for a long time: the waves lapping on the sand were so very easy to listen to.

"I think it's time to go," he said softly.

Up ahead I could see the light. It felt warm and inviting. I pulled my fingers away from Jack's, shaking my head. He looked at me for a very long time before turning and walking off. I watched him until the light seemed to swallow him up.

The water moved around my feet, the sand squishing between my toes as I walked in the other direction.

## The End

# THE SCREECHING OF TWO RAVENS

The Caribbean, England, 1625/1675

Captain Peter Blood stared into the fog that had surrounded his ship for hours. The sea air was heavy and still, just as it had been since shortly after two British men-of-wars had been spotted closing in on the *Arabella*. Minutes later, a fog bank had rolled in out of nowhere, wiping the wind away and wrapping the ship like a heavy grey blanket.

Blood held a small knife in one hand and had been slowly whittling away at a piece of wood he had picked up from one of the ship's carpenter's barrels.

"I've never seen anything like it," muttered Jeremy Pitt, who was standing close to Blood. In the months since they had taken their freedom and the *Arabella*, the former shipmaster had become one of Blood's closest friends. "It's nearly noon and it looks more like dawn, and the ship feels like she hasn't moved an inch. The men are scared, and I don't blame them. But they trust you, Captain, and would sail into a dozen 20-pounders' fire if you asked them to."

The ship was moving, but barely, though it seemed that no one else but Blood had noticed it. He had been letting the shavings from his whittling fall into the water and watching them ever so slowly float, in a single line, back behind the ship. For a long time, there was nothing else, then, in the distance, he could hear the faint crashing of waves on a beach.

"Listen!" he told Pitt.

"Shore?"

"Let's find out. Put one of the longboats into the water and make sure the men are armed. I don't want to put my boots on solid ground and then find out that we are right in the middle of a picnic hosted by our old friend Colonel Bishop, and not be prepared," said Blood.

The fog held the longboat only for a hundred yards before it plunged freely into bright daylight. The shore was only a quarter of a mile ahead,

110

the water slapping against the rocks in rhythmic pulsing. Blood looked back toward the ship but found only a wall of grey fog behind him.

"Make for those large boulders," Blood said. "We'll be sheltered from the wind and away from any prying eyes."

The area looked safe enough, but it was better not to take chances, especially since the only thing Blood knew about where they were was that it wasn't the Caribbean.

"Dodger, you and Harris stay with the long boat," said the Captain as he clambered onto the sand.

"Everyone else, split into two groups; one go north; the other south. Walk for ten minutes, and no more, then come back here," ordered Blood. "Don't get distracted by any local wenches you might see no matter how pretty they are."

"Aye, Captain," the men chorused, several of them laughing. Just being on solid ground seemed to buoy his crew's spirits; even Blood had to admit that he felt better away from the fog.

"Captain," yelled Pitt. "For a moment, I could have sworn there was someone watching us from the ridge. Older man, dark clothes, with a big hat, a staff, and an eye patch. A bird of some kind on his shoulder. But there's no one there now."

Blood motioned for Pitt to follow him. The two men went straight up the slight rise toward the trees, but there was no sign that anyone had been there for a long time.

The wind shifted, moving the trees, while the two men continued to walk. Blood was about to turn back when he stopped. A hundred yards ahead of the two men was a coach turned on its side; one of the two horses that had been pulling it was gone, the other struggling to get on its feet, but held down by the harness. A young man in tan and green livery lay across the front of the coach, sprawled forward like a marionette that had seen its strings cut.

There was a second man on the side of the overturned coach, jabbing his sword through the window at some unseen prey. His back was to Blood, and that was all the advantage that the pirate captain needed. He grabbed the man's leg and yanked, sending him flying off the coach to crash down hard on the ground. Having learned from bitter experience not to turn away from an advantage in a fight, Peter Blood kicked his opponent hard in the ribs, then again in the jaw.

Satisfied that his opponent would not prove any immediate danger, Blood turned his attention back to the coach, climbing onto its side.

"Is anyone there? I'm a doctor; I can help," he said, leaning his face in the window. A moment later he found the barrel of a pistol only an inch or so from his forehead.

"I would not advise you to move, Monsieur," said a stern female voice from the shadows. She held the pistol steadily and the look in her eyes said that, given the slightest provocation, she would fire. "I am not afraid to use this, especially not on an Englishman."

Captain Peter Blood took a deep breath and looked down at the woman who was holding the gun. She was in her mid-20s, her blonde hair was disheveled and her blouse had been ripped in a couple of places.

"Why don't you put that away and let me help you out of there?" said Blood, switching to French, though she did seem to have understood him in English.

"Why don't I just shoot you and then be done with it?" she replied.

"Because that pistol isn't loaded. If it were, I suspect you would have already blown that lout's head off," he said.

The woman looked at him for a moment, then smiled and lowered her head with a brief nod. The pistol vanished and she extended her hand for Blood to take. It was only a matter of a few moments to lift her out of the coach and onto the ground.

The quality of her dress and traveling cape, not to mention her manner, suggested that she was a woman of some position.

"Are you injured?" asked Blood. "I am a doctor."

"A medical man who isn't afraid to get into a bit of a tussle," she said looking at her unconscious attacker.

"One does what one has to," said Blood. "So, would you prefer we speak in English or in French, Madam?"

"English is such a gross language, but I'm a bit out of practice and it could not hurt to refresh my skills," she said. "So may I know the name of my rescuers?"

"Captain Peter Blood; my ship is the *Arabella* out of…the Caribbean," he said. "The other fellow is one of my crewmen, Jeremy Pitt."

"The Caribbean… A large place to call home," she said.

"What can I say," Blood shrugged. "And you are?"

"Clarice de Winter, Baroness Sheffield."

"A pleasure, Milady. May I ask what happened?" said Blood. Though that much was fairly obvious to the captain, he wanted to hear her version of events; that would tell him a lot about his new acquaintance. He was curious to hear her side of it, especially if her tale did not match the one

"I am not afraid to use this."

that he saw around him.

"I was traveling from the estate of my brother-in-law when we were set upon by bandits. My coachman was able to lose them, thanks to some very fine driving on dangerously curved and uneven roads. Regrettably, at the moment that it seemed we had won free from them, the coach wheel hit something and turned over. Then that scum was on us."

"This looks like more than just a happenstance robbery. Were they after something special? I mean, besides the obvious things, gold, assorted loot... yourself?" asked Blood.

"I really don't know what you are talking about, Monsieur. I'm just a traveler who was set on by bandits. They were simply road scum."

If there was one thing about Milady de Winter that Blood noticed at once, beyond her obvious beauty and poise, it was the intelligence behind her eyes. This woman was no vapid bit of smoke, as many noblewomen, he had met before.

"Then why don't we start this conversation over and concentrate on the truth? You are not an idiot, Milady. I think you know why they attacked you."

Her reaction was swift and came without hesitation; she slapped Blood hard on the left side of his face.

"How dare you have the gall to accuse me of lying, Monsieur! Is this the way a gentleman would act? I would have thought better of you. Obviously, I was mistaken."

"Really, Milady? I would expect a somewhat more original reaction from you. Slapping me is so, so predictable."

"And I do hate being predictable," she admitted.

.At that moment, Jeremy Pitt pulled himself up out of the coach, a small leather folio under his arm, which he passed to Blood.

"That is my property and I will thank you to surrender it right now," demanded the Baroness.

There were a dozen or so sheets inside; personal letters, along with two letters of credit that proved the woman in front of him had access to a great deal of money. However, it was the final letter that proved the most interesting; a thick wax seal weighted down the bottom of it as he unfolded the page.

"My written French is a little weak, but this appears to say, 'The bearer of this document is acting on behalf of myself and this office. Give her all cooperation that she requires, without hesitation, under penalty of law. Armand Jean du Plessis, Cardinal Richelieu, state minister to Louis XIII,

King of France.' Impressive credentials, Madame, but a trifle out of date, if I do say so myself," said Blood.

"What do you mean?"

"I admit to not keeping up with the latest news, a bit difficult when you spend a lot of time at sea. But I seem to recall Louis XIII died some years ago, and his son Louis XIV now sits on the throne of France. I'm frankly not sure who this Richelieu fellow might happen to be. The comings and goings of politicians can get quite tiresome after a time."

"The King dead? Hardly! You are misinformed," said Clarice de Winter. "As for Cardinal Richelieu, there are those who say that he is the most powerful man in France. If you will not help me under his authority, perhaps it might be simply a gentleman helping a lady in a time of great distress?"

"So you are trying to appeal to my gentlemanly instinct?" Turning to his companion, Blood said. "Jeremy, do I have any gentlemanly instincts? Now tell the truth."

"I suppose you do when it suits you," said Pitt.

"So, will you help me? I may have spoken too harshly, Captain. There are times when one does not speak in such a way to newly-minted friends," she said softly. "I hope you will accept my apology. I am not a woman who trusts easily, but it appears that I do not have a lot of choices at the moment."

Blood reached down and took her left hand, lifting it to let his lips brush the back of her hand. There was something about this woman's manner, those emerald eyes of hers, that intrigued him, not to mention made him wary as Hell. Under other circumstances, Blood would have enjoyed matching wits with her, and even getting more than a bit physical, in an enjoyable way, but there was still the matter of what they were doing here

"Apology accepted. So why does this Cardinal of yours charge you with so much power? That document could be dangerous in the wrong hands."

"I have, at times, acted as his agent on various matters. A month ago, he charged me to obtain an item for him—a certain wooden box."

"And you chose not to ask why?" questioned Blood.

"With Richelieu, you ask only the things that you need to know in order to carry out the job that has come your way." Clarice de Winter took a few steps toward Blood as if to show she was opening herself to him. "The box was in the hands of a baron named Mannering who is well known for collecting, shall we say, items that are supposed to not even exist."

"I presume that you were able to acquire this box."

"Of course," she replied with a tone that said he should have never doubted that. "The acquiring was not at all difficult, and quite enjoyable," she punctuated her story with a slight smile. "Unfortunately, we were, as you see, intercepted and the box was taken."

"How audacious!" laughed Blood.

Baroness de Winter ignored the tone in Blood's words. "Yes, the Cardinal will not be pleased if I report failure. So, Monsieur, I throw myself on your mercy and ask for your assistance in regaining my property."

"Your property?" Blood arched an eyebrow at the woman and her ideas of ownership.

"Captain, hadn't we better be getting ourselves back to the ship? This whole thing doesn't feel right," argued Pitt.

"No, Jeremy, we're going to assist Milady. The first thing that I want you to do is to help me tie our unconscious friend to yonder tree. Then draw your pistol and hold it at the ready while we have a little discussion with him."

"Aye, Captain!"

Clarice stood back, watching the two men work, a look of satisfaction on her face. "Captain, it may not be necessary for you to question this young man."

Blood arched an eyebrow at her. "Really?"

"Now that I have a look at him, I think I know this face."

The prisoner could not have been more than 15 or 16 years old, hardly older than some enlistees in the navy that Blood had seen, both living and dead.

"You have a wide and diverse group of friends, in that case," said Blood as cheerfully as if he were discussing a beautiful rose bush.

Milady shot the pirate an angry glance. "I saw this man, along with what I presume were his companions in the attack. They came late one night to Mannering's estate, I could never find out why, but I know it was not a pleasant visit, for he was in a foul mood when they left. I did hear one of them say that if he changed his mind, they could be found at the Seven Shadows."

"The Seven Shadows?"

"An inn, a few miles from here."

"Milady, you are a fountain of information," chuckled Blood.

Clarice walked five steps away from Blood and then turned, a small pistol in her hand. She brought the weapon to eye level and aimed at the prisoner. Blood grabbed her hand and twisted the weapon away from her.

"I'm guessing this one is loaded, unlike your other weapon," he said.

"The man was intent on killing me; I simply wanted to make sure that he would have no other chances. If you were more observant, you might have noticed my second gun."

It was Blood's turn to smile this time. He dropped the pistol he had taken from her into his pocket, then reached in beneath her hair and pulled a dagger from a sheath that had been concealed down her back. Blood was fairly sure she had at least two other blades. Not that he had any problem with probing deeper beneath her garments, but Blood felt his point had been made.

"I do not call you a gentleman, good sir," she snarled.

"Call me what you will, just know that, like you, I am observant."

Blood waited a few seconds in the door to allow his eyes to adjust to the inside light. Just before he stepped over the threshold, he heard the screeching of two ravens. The birds were sitting on a fence post and Blood had the unnerving feeling that they were staring directly at him.

The Inn of the Seven Shadows was small but well-maintained, with outbuildings and several corrals. It was more a farm than a traveler's rest stop. Two horses matched Clarice's description of the mounts her attackers had ridden, tied up near the barn. Neither had been allowed to cool down or had been combed out; flecks of lather marked their coats.

"Innkeeper," called Blood as he stepped inside, studying the common area and finding no one in sight. There was an odd silence in the place for a few seconds, then he heard the sound of footsteps coming from a long hallway toward the back of the room.

"Good day, sir. Welcome to our humble abode. How can I be of assistance to a fine gentleman like yourself?" the man said, smiling and eyeing the new arrival warily.

"That all depends on what is in my pocket," Blood said, laying his arm around the shoulders of the innkeeper.

"Sir?" the innkeeper replied, not certain how to take the man's words.

"I have a pistol ball in one pocket and a coin bag in the other. Oh, the pistol ball is in a charged weapon," Blood told him, as casually as if he were speaking of new flowers he had planted, "One of them will be yours. Which would you prefer?"

"The coins," said the man slowly.

"Good choice. Answer me truthfully and they will be yours. Those two horses in your corral, I'm looking for the men who left them. Do you know who they are and where I might find them?"

"They left only an hour ago," the innkeeper stammered, "They were heading east toward the river on a pair of horses they paid me to keep here for them. Milord, I swear as God is my witness that I do not know their names or where they are going. I'm a simple man, trying to keep food on the table for my family."

Blood said nothing, then reached into his pocket, pulled out the coin bag, and dropped a handful of coins into the innkeeper's hands.

"There, that wasn't hard. Now it might be best you forget that I was ever here," he said.

The innkeeper watched Blood disappear out the door before going behind the bar and pulling out a brown bottle. He pulled the cork out of it and swallowed nearly a third of the contents as he heard the sound of a coach rolling away and the screeching of two ravens outside his door.

"There, just to the right!" Blood looked in the direction that Clarice indicated. Just off the road, concealed by bushes, were two nut brown horses; hidden as much by the darkness that had fallen in the last hour as the shrubbery.

"If these do belong to the men we're looking for, I think it best that you remain here, Milady," he told her as he climbed down from the coach.

"Stay here? I think not," replied Clarice, who quickly joined him.

"I think I see a fire, maybe fifty yards inside the tree line," said Pitt.

"Jeremy, I want you to circle around and come in from the east. I think that it might be interesting to see what happens if her ladyship and myself just walk directly into our friends' camp."

The seaman nodded and vanished into the darkness.

"Normally, I would offer you my arm, milady, but in this case, you will stay a few steps behind me, given the circumstances," said Blood.

For once Clarice didn't present an argument, either in word or expression.

Two men were sitting close to the campfire that Jeremy had spotted. Neither reacted nor even seemed to notice Blood's and Clarice's arrival. Before they could get close to the bandits, a grey wolf came out from between the trees and blocked their path.

The animal stared at the two but did not move. Had it not been for the sound of the animal's breathing, Blood could have easily been looking at a prime example of the taxidermist's art.

"Shoot it," said Clarice, her voice low and steady.

"Not yet," said Blood. Out of the corner of his eye he caught sight of a movement among the shadows, one that was gone before he could focus on it.

"No," repeated Blood, he pulled his gun and ran toward the animal, slamming the butt of the weapon t hard against the animal's nose.

The wolf howled and then jerked back before collapsing in a heap. In the darkness, it was hard to say exactly what happened next, but moments later, it was not a wolf that lay on the ground, but a naked boy of perhaps ten or twelve years, clutching his hands to his nose.

"That hurt," he screamed. "I think you broke my nose!"

"It's your own fault, boy!" said a deep-voiced figure, stepping out of the woods near Clarice.

It was the old man that Pitt had said he had seen on the shore: long coat, eye patch, a raven sitting on his shoulder while a second balanced on the head of a walking staff.

"I wasn't going to hurt them, Grandfather," the boy whimpered.

"Fenris, be quiet. You and I both know different," said the old man. "I swear that boy is going to be the death of me one day."

"And you are?" asked Blood.

"I have many names, Dr. Blood, as do you. I think you fully understand the reasons, as I'm sure Baroness de Winter does, herself, or should I call her…"

"Clarice de Winter will be sufficient for this evening," Blood's companion said quickly.

"As you wish, Milady," said the old man. "You may call me Odin, or if you are more comfortable with Merlin, I would answer to that name, as well as a number of others. The boy is my grandson, Fenris."

Blood arched an eyebrow at the old man.

This wasn't the first time that he'd run into someone who thought that he was a god or the anointed spokesman for one; most were gibbering idiots or part of the hierarchy of the Church. Sometimes it was hard to tell them apart.

Yet there was something different in this old man's manner. He had the same kind of intensity Blood had seen on a battlefield, usually by men who, if they didn't survive, would take a lot of their enemies with them.

"If you are who you are implying, then would I be wrong in assuming that you had some hand in what brought my ship here?" asked Blood.

"I have made no claims to being anyone, my dear captain, but it is obvious that you are as astute as I expected you to be. I think we had best be going."

The campfire had faded down to a small glow on the ground in front of the two men. Neither of the bandits looked up or gave any other sign that they were aware of the newcomers. Lying on the ground between them, its lid partially open, was a small wooden box, with a curious design of ivory inlaid on its lid.

"That's it; that's the box that the Cardinal sent me after," said Clarice. "What has it done to these men?"

"Oh, that's simple," laughed Fenris. "They opened it."

"And just opening this box did that?" asked Blood.

"No, it was what was inside, what they saw," Odin clarified. "They saw the future, or what might be the future. Given their reaction, it probably wasn't very pretty. I would imagine it will be days before these two wake up—if they do at all. You never know what kind of animals might decide that these fellows would make a nice midnight snack."

"I suppose you are going to say that you made the box, and want it back," said Blood.

"I want it, but I definitely didn't make it. Let us say that it came from the Middle East and was old when I was a young man. And trust me; that was a very long time ago."

"You are probably lying through your teeth, but if you aren't, then I can see why the Cardinal wants that thing. There are those who would pay a hefty price for that knowledge," said Clarice.

Before either man could react, Clarice de Winter picked up the box and lifted the lid letting a sickly dull yellow glow appear. When she did that, her face went as pale as one who had left the land of the living. That Milady was not a woman who frightened easily had been obvious to Blood from the first moment he met her, but at that moment, he read pure terror and confusion on her face.

Blood grabbed the box away from her, snapping it closed.

"Are you all right?" asked Blood. "Did you see something?"

"I saw darkness," she whispered, rubbing her neck, her fingers clinging there as if to protect herself from some unseen attack. "There was a sudden searing pain and then darkness."

Fenris' laughter was enough to drag Blood's attention away from his companion. "I think you had best give it to me; that's what I'm here for. Or I might have to eat you." The boy went to all fours and his transformation back into a wolf was too fast to follow. A deep, frightening growl emerged from the animal's throat just as Blood fired and Odin drove his walking staff hard against his grandson's side. The smoke from the pistol, the painful scream from the animal combined with the screeching of the ravens, and it was over in a matter of seconds.

"Is he dead?" asked Blood.

"Hardly," said Odin, his voice weak for only a moment. "Let's just say that he is going to have one mighty headache when he wakes up. He will definitely be in a very foul mood and hard to control. I suggest it is time for you to retire to more congenial climes."

"And get there how?"

Odin reached up to his shoulder and coaxed one of the ravens onto his hand. He whispered something to it and then the bird flew toward Blood and landed on the pirate's shoulder.

"My friend will show you the way."

"So, you got lost," said Blood.

Jeremy Pitt turned away from his captain and walked over to the edge of the deck, spending several minutes making sure that several lines were tied fast.

"Are you ever going to let me forget that?" he asked finally, a note of exasperation in his voice.

"Eventually, I suppose I will," smiled Blood.

He had found Jeremy wandering around the forest a few minutes after leaving Odin and Fenris. Together the two of them had bundled Clarice de Winter into the coach. She was still in something of a stupor, muttering half-finished sentences. They had left her, along with the coach, at the Inn of the Seven Shadows. The innkeeper had not been pleased with his new guest but seemed to accept that he had no choice in the matter.

"When she comes round, I have every confidence that she will spin a tale for this Cardinal which attaches no blame to her for not getting him his prize," Blood had told Pitt as they left.

On the beach, they found Odin's raven perched on the edge of the long boat. Almost as soon as the shore party had returned to the *Arabella*, the wind had shifted to let the ship move seaward. In what seemed less than an hour they breached the fog and were again in familiar Caribbean waters.

"Good day, Captain," said a familiar voice.

Odin standing next to him did not surprise Peter Blood; if it had, he would not have given the old man the satisfaction of knowing it.

"You?" Jeremy Pitt made no attempt to hide the surprise on his face when he saw the old man.

"Me," nodded Odin.

"Somehow, I think the Caribbean is somewhat far from your usual haunts," Blood said casually.

"True, though my followers have been known to venture into this part of the world in the past," said the old man. "However, I've come because we have some unfinished business."

Blood cocked his head at Odin. "And what would that be?"

"I brought you to France for one reason. I could not seize the box myself, because of, shall we say, my nature. It has to be freely given to me. Neither Milady de Winter, the Cardinal, nor Baron Mannering were likely to do so. That's why I chose you."

"And now you want it. Jeremy, go below to my cabin and get the small leather bag, you know the one, it's on the floor under my work table."

"Aye, sir," Jeremy Pitt muttered.

"Given what it can do to people, it is best that the box be hidden away. The consequences of opening it might be catastrophic," said Odin.

"And you can be trusted with it? I have known a number of Norse and Swedes; the tales they tell of Odin don't inspire that much trust in you."

"I could say the same thing about the tales they tell of you, Captain Blood. In only six months, you have become quite the notorious pirate. So, you well know how a certain kind of reputation can work to one's advantage. I'm sure you've encouraged the spreading of somewhat exaggerated stories concerning your exploits."

That was true, Blood had to admit. Reputations were strange things, half-truth, half-dream with a generous drop of confusion mixed into the batter.

Pitt reappeared with the bag and passed it to Blood, who looked at it for a moment. Then, with all his might, he sent the thing flying out over the ocean. It struck the water, lingered on the surface for a moment, and then vanished into the clear Caribbean depths.

"I think the best keeper for that thing, whatever it might really be, is in the hands of Davy Jones. It's not that I don't trust you, sir, but to be frank, I don't trust you or anyone with that thing," Blood said.

Odin chewed on his lip for a moment. Blood waited for his legendary fury to make itself known, but instead, the old man smiled and then laughed.

"Checkmate, Captain Blood. I must admit that was not an action that I had anticipated. Well played, my friend."

Odin gestured toward the raven that had been quietly watching the whole affair from his perch on a wooden barrel. The bird hesitated, then leaped into the air and flew straight to Odin's wrist.

"Captain, may I wish you smooth sailing and strong winds at your back." Then he was gone as if he had never stood on the deck next to Blood.

The pirate captain stood there for a moment and began to laugh.

## The End

# Money's Worth

I had my hand on the dagger before I was fully awake. Sleeping with a knife under your pillow isn't the most comfortable thing to do, though you can get used to it. I'd rather be uncomfortable than wake to a sword at my throat.

When I leased the villa last month the caretaker had apologized profusely about the number of things that needed fixing; after all, the place had been empty for nearly two years.

One of the problems he had mentioned was the hinges on the master bedroom door; they squeaked and needed replacing. He had sworn by any number of local gods that he would have it fixed quickly.

It hadn't been. Right then I didn't have a problem with those squeaky hinges. They had been enough to awaken me.

There were two intruders, small hunkered forms clinging far too closely together as they came across the floor. When they sprang I threw my blanket over them as I rolled over the other side of the bed.

"So what enemies have tried to ambush me?" I demanded, my voice as melodramatic as possible since I already knew the identities of these intruders. I threw the blanket aside and fought hard to suppress a grin at the scene in front of me, a jumble of legs, arms, and tangled hair, mixed in with gasps and giggles. "Is it some demon or perhaps an advance scout for the Kelmigie Horde? Whatever foul creature it is I will crush it under my heel and serve the remnants to the dogs!"

"No!" The bundle of arms and legs separated into two forms and scrambled madly toward the far side of the bed.

Kellian was eight; his sister Jayce was two years younger but nearly as tall. Their red hair came from my side of the family. Their chaotic nature was a legacy from both their father and myself.

"It's us, Mother," Kellian yelled.

"Really it is," his sister added.

"I don't know! Those could be very good disguises. You could de dwarfs from the deep mines. I'd best beat you severely, just in case."

Jayce turned to her brother. "I told you this was a bad idea, that Mommy would be mad and punish us."|

I wasn't mad; I was quite pleased with the two of them. They had been at each other's throats for the last several days, over some incident that they had both forgotten by now. That they had made peace and decided to attack me was a good sign.

"Mother, we were just playing! We thought it would be fun to play Kyber assassins!" Kellian proclaimed.

Kyber assassins?! It didn't surprise me that they had heard of the Kyber Guild.

There were half a hundred tall tales about the Guild, told by children and adults to frighten each other, most all of them far, far from the truth.

Nothing in my possession had the Guild name on it; only a seal, hidden away in a compartment in one of my trunks even bore the emblem.

"All right! I believe you aren't dwarves wearing a disguise spell to make me think you are my children. I will let you off, this time, young Kybers." I picked up a piece of fruit from the table next to my bed and broke it into several smaller sections. "But only if you help me eat this. Do you agree to my terms?"

"Yes!"

Six weeks ago I had announced that I was taking an extended holiday, officially to escape the seasonal heat in the capitol, as were many others who could afford to move to the mountains or the sea for a few months. Unofficially, I just needed some time away from not just the Kyber Guild but the various businesses I ran as a part of my "every day" identity.

I had chosen Yallon's Bay because it was several days' travel from the capitol, far enough away for some privacy but close enough not to be completely out of touch.

Of course, this was not the first time I had come to Yallon's Bay; that had been a decade and a half before with my beloved Micah.

Here he was remembered as one of the five thousand men lost in the Battle of Summer Falls. I had no intention of disillusioning anyone about that tale; besides, who would want to hear that he had died in an attempt to assassinate General Zyon, one of our officers who had defected to the other side? I preferred to let our "friends" think of Micah as a dead war hero and myself as a rich, respectable widow.

The downside of Yallon's Bay was several "social" obligations that I would cheerfully have ignored; however, attending them was part of my public persona.

"Lady Danya, it is most gratifying to see you again," Lord Junius had said as I arrived at his home for what had been billed as a small gathering. Conservatively, I estimated that, excluding servants, there were well over fifty other guests: humans, dwarves, and elves, along with a smattering of other races.

"Danya, are you all right?"

I turned to look at Cyma Tamu, her thin face furrowed as if she was uncertain of what she wanted to hear me answer. She was an inquisitive sort, but Cyma did have the good sense to know some questions were best left unasked.

I realized that I had been staring out at the bay, studying the ships. Three new ones had arrived on the morning tide. They were small, compared to the large merchant men more common near the capitol. But Yallon's Bay was off the major trade routes and too shallow to take the really large vessels.

"Oh, it's nothing, Cyma," I said. "It was just seeing the bay right now, something about the way the light is falling on it reminded me of the first time that Micah and I came here."

I let a long sigh write a look of nostalgia on my face. Let Cyma take whatever interpretations of it that came to her mind; she was very good at that. Truth be told, Micah and I had first come here seeking a hideout. A mission for the Guild had gone wrong and we needed to be someplace where no one knew us.

That had been a good time. For a moment I let myself miss Micah more than I had in a long time.

"Now, Danya, you must accept the fact that Micah is gone. Remember always, he died a hero of the Empire; that is something that you and the children can be proud of. While I didn't know him, I have the feeling that he wouldn't want you to lose yourself mourning for him forever. You are still young and very beautiful."

I smiled. "Beautiful, hardly; but thank you, Cyma."

"You are definitely beautiful, don't deny it," she laughed. "In case you haven't noticed, someone can't take his eyes off you."

"Indeed?" I asked, searching my memory for any recent arrivals that I was not aware of.

"Oh yes." Cyma gestured toward a tall man, dressed in silken finery, at the far end of the room. Even at this distance, I could see the marks of Elvin blood in him - silver-streaked hair, long fingers, and a narrow face.

"Interesting," I said

"He's been asking about you," Cyma said, a slight purr in her words.

"Does he not have the courage to come and face me himself?"

"Who knows what will happen? This gathering has at least several more hours of life in it. Then there is the rest of the night." The suggestive purr was back in Cyma's voice.

"Indeed." I admit I was a bit intrigued. I looked back to where he was standing but the man was nowhere in sight.

An hour later I found myself back at the balcony, having made a half transit of the room, speaking with a number of my neighbors, letting them see the "me" that I wanted known around the town. It would be a bit longer before I could withdraw and return home without committing a social faux pas.

I caught sight of the stranger only twice, always at a distance. It seemed an odd little dance the two of us were doing.

The sun had begun to disappear over the horizon, letting dusk streak itself across the waters of the bay as the three-quarter moon appeared in the sky. The full moon would come in a day or so.

"Is the wind from the south, Lady Sable?" It was my admirer stepping up beside me. His words were pitched low, intended for me alone.

"Pardon me, m'lord?"

"Is the winds from the south, Lady Sable?"

I was a little taken aback. No one should have known my Guild name, let alone that phrase, in Yallon's Bay.

"Ask about the weather and it will change in a blink."

Sign, countersign.

"How do you know me?" I demanded.

"The Widow told me," he said. "After the proper payments, of course. I hope I get my money's worth."

I wanted to turn and walk away. This man knew far too much about me for my liking.

"Very well, but this is not the place to talk. There are too many ears attached to wagging tongues," I said.

It wasn't that I wanted to hear what he had to say, or, frankly, gave a damn. I just didn't want anyone else hearing it.

Besides, I was not happy at his being here at all. Of course, knowing The Widow, enough money would make her forget my decree. She also knew, of course, that I would say no; that is an option all of us have. I'd been very specific about my wishes; but the Guild would have the money, the introduction fee was non-refundable.

"Fear not, I've laid a minor glamour around us. All anyone will hear will be whispers that no one can quite make out and none will approach, thinking it a near romantic tryst," He reached up and took my hand. He didn't lean forward and kiss it, just did a slight bow.

"You are prepared."

"I try"

"I need you to kill someone, and it must be soon."

No big surprise there. "First, there are some niceties to be observed, m'lord," I told him. "The courtesy of your name would be a good start, though I suspect I could find it out easily from any one of a dozen people around us."

"My name is not necessary. The only name you need is that of she whom I want you to kill."

"On the contrary, it is very necessary. You have sought me out, at some great expense if I know The Widow. Obviously, you know who and what I am."

"A killer," he said with certainty in his voice. "As are all the Kyber Guild."

"Understand this," I said. "I know of five ways to kill you, where you stand, without even breaking a sweat or staining my clothing with blood. Three of them would look like you had just died a natural death. So shall we start again?"

I could see him thinking, wondering just how far to take my challenge to him, wondering perhaps just how far I would go right now.

"Very well. I am Rathbin of the House of De Costa." I vaguely knew the family name, one of the lesser Elvin houses, too much human blood for the High Houses to give them more than the briefest acknowledgment, too much elf blood to "fit in" as more than a token among the higher born human clans.

"See, that didn't hurt at all," I said.

De Costa scanned the garden just below us. He gestured toward the far end where I could see a woman, dressed in a fur-edged cape.

"That is her, your target. Her name is Layra. She is my sister."

On more than one occasion I had heard my children threaten to kill each other, but the next moment they would be laughing and playing together. De Costa was taking sibling rivalry a good way further along the track than normal.

"I must decline your offer."

De Costa's face went paler than it had been, then ran red with anger. 'What! You can't! She must die by your hand!"

"Not by my hand. Do it yourself if you are that adamant. I decline. I'm on holiday; there is no argument that will persuade me otherwise"

He grabbed me, his face a grim mask of hate, long finger tightening around my arm. "It must be you!"

With my free hand, I slapped him hard and then drove my knee into his groin. That was more than enough to get him to let go of me. I stepped away and saw him draw back, my unexpected attack being quite effective.

Despite the glamour that de Costa had cast, that little exchange caught more then a few people's attention.

Cyma came running up. "Are you all right?"

"Lord de Costa just needs to learn that when I say no, I mean no."

I left Cyma doing what she did so well, drawing the wrong conclusion.

Over the next two days I saw de Costa a half dozen times, always silently staring with the same grim face. I didn't give a rat's ass if he wanted his sister dead, I just couldn't figure out why he insisted that I had to be the one to do it.

That was why, two hours after sunset, on the third night since the party, I was sitting, concealed in the branches of a tree just outside of his house.

I had plumbed certain local sources to find out what I could about the man. It turned out not to be much. He had come from the south, but no one knew exactly where, arriving in Yallon's Bay a month before, having purchased the house through an agent earlier in the year. That proved he had money, but I knew that since even a chat with The Widow can cost an arm and a leg, not to mention your firstborn.

What bothered me was that there was even less to discover about his sister than about de Costa, save that she lived only a mile from her brother. There was endless speculation, but no hard facts.

I had taken to my bed early in the afternoon, complaining of a sour stomach, leaving instructions that I was not to be disturbed. If anyone looked into my bedroom they would see a figure enshrouded in heavy blankets.

De Costa had spent most of the evening in the house's library, studying some documents and books that looked very old. Just before midnight he finally blew out the last candle and left the room. I remained on my perch for a slow count of a thousand before dropping onto the balcony outside his window.

....dropping onto the balcony....

Once inside I lit a small candle and put it into the metal holder I had brought; the shutters could be opened one at a time to direct the light where I wanted and to keep it to a minimum

I sat down and began to study what he had left behind. The books were old and had the smell of ages on them. One of them left the palm of my hand tingling after I touched it. I could make out only a single word embossed on the cover, _Aubic._

There were also loose papers, written in a clear concise hand, spread over the desktop; most were business dealings, nothing personal.

"I think you might find something interesting in the lower right-hand drawer, Lady Sable." A section of the bookcase on the far side of the room had swung open. De Costa stood there, a much too satisfied look on his face.

Damn it! I would have read the riot act to any first-year apprentice who didn't check for hidden doors when they invaded a room.

"Good evening, Lord de Costa. I get the feeling that you were expecting me. I presume that you've got a spell on the chair to keep me from getting up."

"Actually, no," he said leaning against the bookcase frame. "But before you decide to bolt or to use any number of those skills that I know you possess, I think you really should look at what is in the drawer."

I rose slightly, just to test his words, and could feel no restraints, sorcerous or otherwise. It would only be a matter of a few seconds to get me out of the window.

Opening the drawer, I found a wooden casket. The wood was smooth, almost silky to the touch. The hinge and latches were almost impossible to find; whoever had made it had been a master craftsman. I doubted that there would be any sort of contact poison. That seemed to be a far cry from what de Costa had in mind.

Inside was a silver blade laying on a red silk piece of cloth. Two glyphs were emblazed on the blade; I recognized one of them as a Dakarian Moon, the other I did not know but even the sight of it sent a shiver down my spine.

"A Moon Dagger?"

Moon Daggers were few and far between; no more than a dozen were even rumored to exist. They were said to have been forged from sky metal by a Dwarven smith nearly a hundred years ago for an order of sorcerers that had been destroyed in the Three Sabers War.

I personally knew where six of them were; safely buried under several tons of rock in the ruins of the Fulgrham temple. If this happened to be one of those, then there was a lot more to de Costa than I thought.

"I searched for more than a decade after I first learned of them," he said. "Then one day I saw it lying on a fishmonger's table. He accepted a rather large payment and never knew what he had."

"Some people have all the luck."

"I want you to use it this very night."

"On you, perhaps?"

"I'm sure that would please you to no end. Before you try, I would suggest that you look at what else is inside that casket." He moved over to a bookcase and picked up a small statuette, running one hand across its surface.

I lifted the cloth and found a pair of small hand mirrors. De Costa nodded, indicating that this was what I was looking for. Hefting one of them I stared deep into it and felt my heart drop out of me.

Instead of my reflection, I saw my daughter. She was asleep. In the other one, I saw my son. Both children were seemingly undisturbed. A small dark spot hovered over each, gradually shifting form into that of a dagger, identical to the one lying in front of me.

"Those are echoes of the Moon Dagger. I assure you that neither of those fine young people will come to any harm, they will simply sleep the night away," said de Costa. "Provided you do as I have requested. The spell that I am weaving will require the heart blood of the house of de Costa. You have two hours to plunge that blade into my sister's heart. If you don't, those blades in the mirror will plunge into your children's hearts."

"You slimy bastard." It took all my concentration to control myself. Losing my temper would not save my children. "I should use this on you."

"I wouldn't. I crafted the spell so that should anything happens to me, then the knives do their work," he said casually. "As for my sister, with her defenses, I can't enter her sanctum, nor she mine, without an invitation. Trust me; neither of us is going to be issuing the other one of those. Now, be on your way, the moon is full. I need her blood spilled with the dagger while the moon is full."

He picked up the two mirrors and looked into their surfaces, smiling.

Given the minimal amount of time involved, there was no way to plan a quiet way into the house of de Costa's sister, so I opted for something simple and straightforward— I went in the front door.

It wasn't barred and there was no sign of any guards. Given the siblings' magical interests, that didn't surprise me, any more than the distinct feeling that I was being watched from the moment I crossed the threshold.

If I believed de Costa, then his sister would be asleep in the master bedroom, toward the rear of the house. He seemed to think that I should be able to waltz right in, carve her like a goose and wander away at my leisure. I, on the other hand, had my doubts about that plan.

"Why don't we have a drink and talk about it?"

I had barely stepped into her bedroom when Layra de Costa spoke. Like her brother, she seemed able to turn up when no one expected her.

It took a moment for me to locate her, sitting in a large throne-like chair just to the right of the bed.

"I'm not going to insult you by assuming that you don't know why I'm here," I said.

"Lady Sable, you're quite direct. I like that." That she knew my Guild name made me wonder just how many people had paid The Widow for information about me.

I suppose I expected Layra de Costa to make some sort of magical gesture and conjure up a globe of light or some such thing as that. Instead, I heard the very distinctive sound of flint being struck, followed by sparks and a shard of wood glowing as its tip burst into flame.

She held it out to the wicks of several candles nearby; the light was enough for me to see her face. Layra de Costa wore green, so dark it was almost black. Her silver-streaked hair spilled loosely over her shoulders. I could see the resemblance to her brother.

"Half-brother, actually; our father, shall we say, got around a bit and had a taste for human women. In our cases, two different human women," she said.

"Interesting, you can read minds." That would be all I'd need in someone I had come to kill.

"Not actually; it just seemed a logical thing that you might wonder," she said.

Simple and straightforward, I liked that. I reminded myself that no matter how much I might like her; there was the matter of those two ghostly daggers hanging over my children.

"Did he at least provide you with a reason that he wants me dead?" Layra said, pouring two glasses of wine and passing one to me.

I waited until she had taken a sip before lifting my own, not that I drank from it, but there are ways of appearing to.

"Nothing specific, something about tapping the power of your late father, though he did give me some damn good motivation to follow through on his wishes/" I held my hand on the pommel of the Moon Dagger, its metal now ice cold to the touch, letting her see the weapon.

"Did you see a very old book, with the word Aubic on the cover?"

I nodded and mentioned the fact that touching it had left my hand tingling.

"Our father's grimoire; then it is obvious that my dear brother has broken the seal and found the spells that were the source of our late father's power. From what our parents said, it would require the blood of our family to do such a casting," she said.

"Wouldn't your father have had to have a Moon Dagger to do it in the first place?"

Layra reached down to the side of her chair and brought out a blade identical to the one I held.

"He had one," she said.

"It figures," I muttered, then I let fly with the Moon Dagger.

I probably should have been a lot more discreet, given the large bag I was carrying, when I went back to de Costa's villa. I wasn't in the mood for subtlety; I just wanted to make sure my children were not within reach of his slimy fingers one minute more than they had to be.

De Costa was behind his desk when I entered. "Welcome, Lady Sable, welcome," he said. "I trust all went well and as I requested."

"It did, and I have brought you proof of my deed." I laid the bag down on the floor, near the bookcase with the sliding panel. Very carefully I untied the ropes at the top and pulled it open. In the dim light, Layra's face was pale as her head rolled lifeless to one side.

"Unnecessary; her blood on the Moon Dagger would have been sufficient. If you felt you had to bring proof I would have been happy with just her head," he said. "Oh, sweet sister, I've never been more pleased to see you." For a moment it was as if the two of them were alone in the room.

De Costa came around the desk and toward the body. I stepped in between him and his goal.

"Hold it right there. You get her, and I frankly don't care what you do with her," I said. "But only when you fulfill your end of the bargain by taking those ghost daggers from my children's throats!"

I watched his jaw tighten as he stared at me, unblinking. I already knew that he wasn't used to people telling him what to do, and didn't like it when it happened, but I didn't care. I was prepared to do some serious damage to him if that was what was necessary to keep the children safe.

"Very well, Lady Sable," he said, at last, his voice as casual as if talking about the time of day rather than children's lives. "You did as I asked and my word is my bond."

De Costa went back to the desk and picked up the casket that the Moon dagger had been in. I could see the two mirrors from where I stood and I felt a tug at my heart seeing the vague forms in them that were my son and daughter.

Holding the mirrors in one hand, he smashed them down against the corner of the desk. Shards of glass flew everywhere. For a moment I felt like I could see the forms of the blades over the pieces of glass, then they dissipated.

I wanted that to be the end of it. But what you want and what happens are often two different things.

"As promised, both of your little darlings are safe," he announced.

"One thing," I said.

"Our bargain is completed. Your Guild will have its fee, and you have your children. What more is there to say?"

"There is more," I continued, ignoring his attitude. "Why me when there are any numbers of street thugs, mercenaries, even other Kybers you could have hired? Why did you insist on me?"

De Costa laughed: it was a sickening cackle. "The night I acquired the Moon Dagger I had a vision: my sister, dead, the hand that had wielded the blade was yours. You were a key pivot point to achieving my destiny. Does that satisfy your curiosity?"

I nodded and stepped to one side. I've dealt with any number of magic users over the years. The necromancers like him left me repulsed. Kneeling beside her, the man moved the cloth further away from her head, and then gently ran his fingers along her hair.

"Not that you weren't planning to do this to me, Layra. You shall bring our father's power to his rightful heir, me."

De Costa grabbed the bag and began to rip it down the center, revealing Layra's blood-stained blouse right over her heart. I caught myself wondering if the man knew where that was; he certainly didn't seem to have one.

Even with his back to me, I could tell when he realized that something was wrong.

"The Dagger, where is it?" He screeched in an almost feminine voice. "I will need it to finish this night's work."

"Oh, is this what you want?" I asked innocently, holding the blade up.

"I think not, brother," said Layra. Her eyes were open, a look of pure hatred on her face. Since she couldn't enter the house without an invitation, I gave her one. It wasn't that I didn't trust de Costa fully to keep his side of the bargain, but it pays to have a backup plan.

Layra brought out the other Moon Dagger. Her aim was good; as close as she was to her brother, it would have been hard to miss. The blade drove easily through cloth, flesh and bone, and into de Costa's heart.

I could tell when the shock passed and pain swallowed Rathbin de Costa. Blood began to run around the edges of the blade, spewing out after a few moments to strike Layra, the furniture, and even me. He trembled and then collapsed backward.

Layra sister struggled out of the bag and to her feet. She stared at her brother for a time and then began to chant. I couldn't understand the words; there are more dialects of elfish than there are grains of sand in the desert.

Any possibility that it might be a mourning chant passed quickly. I could feel the magic stirring in the air around me. I realized she was doing exactly what her brother had planned. I had the feeling that this was not a good thing. She had known more than she had let on.

Vague images formed in the air above the body, most of them things that I did not want to even put a name to. But when I saw Killian and Jayce there, I knew what I had to do.

I stepped up behind Layra, threw my arm around her neck, and brought the Moon Dagger around. This time it did not strike into the chair to one side of her, as it had earlier, but drove directly up under her rib cage and into her heart.

"I could ha…."

That was all she got out before the light faded from her eyes. I let go of her and she fell into the arms of her brother.

"I guess you got your money's worth," I told the dead sorcerer.

# The End

# WIND AND SHADOW

It was going to rain. Michael knew that as certainly as he could see the thin line of clouds and the moon hanging over the horizon. There hadn't been a word about rain in the television weather; he just knew it would happen, probably within an hour.

The pale moonlight bathed the whole area, making the cemetery gate almost luminescent. Michael smiled slightly as he read it, Floral Haven Cemetery. How many times had he driven past this place since he had gotten his license, or come to watch them put family members and friends into the ground?

The moonlight was enough to help pick a path across the gravel road and between the few thin trees that stood as narrow shadows above the ground-hugging tombstones.

It had been three hours since the funeral.

He had been there, though not among the crowd gathered around the gravesite; preferring to watch from the protection of the abandoned convenience store across the street from the cemetery. Once the limos and their cars were gone, that had been when he had known it was his time to visit the grave.

Michael hadn't said anything to make the grave diggers stop. They just looked up, saw him, backed a respectful distance away, and then headed off toward the maintenance building. Latecomers at a graveside funeral service were a normal sight for someone who worked at a cemetery. It was also an excuse for a cigarette break, so they disappeared quickly.

Standing next to the coffin, he hadn't been sure just what he should be thinking or remembering just then. Finally, Michael reached over and put his hand on the cold metal next to the flower spray of white and red roses.

"Goodbye, Dad, I love you."

He'd known all along that there would be one more visitor; that was the reason for the vigil. The sound of footsteps coming from behind him proved him right.

"When did they say that the marker would be put in?" asked the newcomer.

"According to the funeral home people, the permanent one won't be ready for several weeks. They're supposed to have a temporary one in place in the next day or two," said Michael.

"Good. It's nice to see you, Michael."

"I wondered when you would hit town, James. Where were you when you got word about Dad?" said his brother.

"Seattle."

"Seattle? I thought you didn't like coffee."

"Times change, kiddo. You still down in the Big Easy?"

"You know it," said James. "It's definitely my kind of town."

"I really need to get down there for a visit. You can show me the decadent underbelly of the place."

"Like I would know it?"

"Like you wouldn't?" said Michael.

"True," laughed James. "I noticed it didn't take you long to get out of Tulsa and not look back."

"I may have been born here, but that didn't mean I have to stay here," said Michael. Michael looked at his brother. The two of them had not stood face to face in nearly ten years. Yet in that time, James seemed not to have changed, though his face was paler than his brother recalled. Michel didn't need the mirror to show him the changes in his face; gray in the hair, more and more lines around the eyes and mouth. That was quite a difference for brothers born only a year apart.

"Were you at the funeral?" asked James.

"No," Michael sighed. "I watched from across the way. I really didn't feel like putting up with our dear relatives." Michael gave a dry chuckle. "I'm sure that just added grist to the mill of their gossiping about what a disgrace to the family I was and all the heartache I caused Dad."

"I figured you would have been there, if for no other reason than just to irritate them."

"I considered it. Dad would have enjoyed that. But I just couldn't. I had enough of them up at the hospital. At least I got to see him before he died."

"Yeah, that's what was important, seeing him," said James.

"The night I got back into town I went straight to the hospital. A half-dozen of our cousins and aunts were holding court in Dad's room. You would have thought that Death itself had come walking in among them the way they looked at me. You should have heard dear Aunt May, so condescending it made my stomach turn. After all, as if dying weren't enough, her "poor brother" now had to put up with having his gay son waltz in and annoy him," said Michael.

"There are times when I wonder why Dad ever claimed her and the rest of that sorry-assed bunch of relatives of ours. The only thing they were interested in from him was his money and political contacts. How do you think they would have reacted if they had seen me?" James reached into his jacket and pulled out a cigar case, along with a box of old-fashioned wooden matches.

"Considering that most of them were at your funeral, I imagine not well at all."

James' tombstone was not a dozen steps from where the two of them stood. Michael remembered the shock when, two days after his brother's funeral, he had found James standing on the balcony of his apartment.

"Yeah, well, I'm not surprised, considering some of our relatives. At least Dad accepted me, and you. I know that it couldn't have been easy for him." He took a long draw on the cigar and then let the smoke out slowly.

"Hey, first he finds out that one son is gay, and then he finds out that the other one has become a vampire. Not that either of us had much choice in the matter. He was a strong man; he had to be. I'd like to think that we both inherited a share of that strength," said Michael.

"So, what did Dad say to you when you talked to him?"

"And what makes you think that I was even there? How do you know I didn't just get in from Seattle a few hours ago and drive straight here?"

"James, this is me you're talking to, so cut the crap. I don't know just how long you've actually been here in town, but I know that you were here before Dad died. I know you, and I know that nothing what-so-ever could have kept you from here, unless you were dead, too."

"Michael, in case you haven't noticed, I am dead. I've even got the paperwork to prove it," James told his brother.

"Your point?"

James chuckled. "You certainly have a lot of faith in me, little brother."

"Hey, I saw how you got out of trouble when you were dating the Delvechio triplets, all at the same time. Anyone who could do that can accomplish almost anything."

Of course, what Michael hadn't mentioned to his brother was a conversation he had had with a third-shift nurse at the hospital the night before his father died. That nurse had told him about someone showing up very late to see him; the picture of James in Michael's wallet had been enough to identify him.

"You're right." James blew out several smoke rings, then dropped the cigarillo, stubbing it out on the dirt. "We did talk, for nearly an hour. He seemed pleased when I came into the room. We said goodbye. I think we both knew that was what was happening."

Michael took a deep breath and held it. Shifting his weight to one side, Michael rammed his elbow hard into James' side. The blow was so unexpected that James bent forward, a gasp of air hanging in front of his face. As swiftly as the first blow, Michael struck his brother again, the force knocking him to the ground.

"What the Hell is the matter with you, Michael? Are you insane? He demanded.

Michael knew what he had to do and do it quickly. James was stronger than four men, and unbelievably fast, so he knew he had only a few seconds.

"Oh, I'm very, very sane, kiddo, maybe more so than I've ever been." Michael drove the flat of his hand hard against James' chin, then jammed the point of his heavy boot into James' knee and then his groin.

James' face went paler as he struggled for breath. "Why?"

"You know as well as I do. Because of him. Because of Dad."

"Dad?"

"You could have saved him. But you let him die!"

"Save him?"

"Yes, you asshole. Save him! You could have made him like you are. He didn't have to die."

James struggled to his feet, back arched like an animal ready to spring. "What makes you think that I didn't offer?"

At that, James threw himself hard against his brother, the impact staggering the two of them. Both men struggled to remain on their feet, hands grasping at each other in a blink struggle. In an instant, it was over. Michael found himself yanked away from his brother.

"Damn it, boys! Stop it, both of you!"

The voice was familiar, all too familiar, yet both brothers knew that it was impossible. Standing between Michael and James, dressed in tan slacks and a dark blue flowered Hawaiian shirt that he had bought one day to annoy his wife, was their father, Saul.

"Dad?"

Saul Gideon stared at his sons, slowly shaking his head. Looking at him, Michael realized that his father was standing on two good legs, which was astounding, since a year before his death, Saul's left leg had been amputated because of a diabetic infection.

"It hasn't changed since the two of you were tiny. You're either trying to beat the daylights out of each other or be each other's best friend. Are you two ever going to grow up? I'm not going to be around to pull you two apart anymore," he said.

Saul reached into his pocket and pulled out a cigar. Without taking his eyes off his two sons, he unwrapped the stogie and stuck it in his mouth. Ever so slowly the end began to glow red and a thin line of smoke emerged. He looked ten - no, fifteen – years younger than he had when he died.

"Dad, didn't the doctor tell you that you had to quit smoking? It's bad for you," James said.

"Somehow, I doubt that it will bother me much now," chuckled Saul. The older man took a long draw of the cigar, obviously savoring the taste. Michael realized that parts of his father were more solid than others; he could see through the man's chest, but not his arms or face. He also looked no older than forty, though Michael knew he was sixty-five.

"Dad, don't take this wrong, but you're dead." He gestured at the coffin.

"Ya think? Is believing in your father as a ghost any more difficult than believing your brother is a vampire? Look, I don't have all that long here. There are places that I should be, but I had the feeling that I would need to be here one more time."

Saul walked along the edge of his grave. Behind him, that moon had been covered by more and more clouds. Michael noticed that the smell of rain was heavy in the air.

"So, what were you going to do, Michael, after you had beaten the daylights out of your brother? Maybe hold him down until you could drive a stake through his heart?" Asked Saul.

"Maybe; probably not. I just wanted to make him hurt, for not saving you," said Michael.

For a moment, Saul's face showed all of his sixty-five years but then shifted back to the younger iteration. "Thank you, Michael; not for what you were going to do, but for caring enough to think you had to do something. I know you were hurting, but you didn't have to do something like that. That last night in the hospital, James offered to make me like him. I said no."

"Why not, Dad?"

"Because I was just tired. Ten years of pain, a slow creeping kind that never gave me a minute's peace, was the reason. When we lost your mother last year; that was the moment I knew that I didn't want to go on without her."

"I knew you felt that way, but I had to give you the chance, a way out if you wanted it," James said. "And the same offer is open to you, little brother, if you want it. This isn't an easy life, but it is a life."

Michael embraced his brother, not sure what his feelings were right then.

"Now, will you two promise me there won't be any more knockdown drag outs?"

"Can't promise that, Dad," said Michael, a half smile on his face. "But let's just say there won't be any more tonight."

"James?"

"What Michael said."

"Good. I won't be seeing either one of you for a very long time. I want you both to know that I'm proud of you. I've always loved you both." He reached into his shirt and pulled out a pocket watch. "Yipes, I'm late. Your mother is probably wondering where I am, and if I don't get a more on she will be madder than Hell."

As suddenly as he had come, Saul Carter was gone, leaving nothing but Michael's and James' memories in his wake.

"I don't know about you, but I could use a drink right now," said Michael.

James pulled a metal flask out of his inside coat pocket and passed it over to Michael, who unscrewed the top and took a swallow, a moment later gasping for breath.

"Kiddo, that's something," he said, handing it back slowly. "Please tell me there wasn't any blood mixed in there."

"No. Why would I waste that on you? That's nothing but good old Kentucky whiskey. So, kiddo, are you any better with a pool cue than you used to be?"

"Good enough to beat the stuffing out of you."

"I don't think Dad would object to you trying that," James said.

"I don't think he would, either. Michael grinned and wrapped his arm around his brother's shoulder.

"So," James said. "How's about we head for the Sho-Bar and find out?"

"You have been gone a while. They turned the Sho-Bar into a CYW place about a year ago."

"Yuck! That is an offense against the natural order of the universe!"

"The Gold Dragon is still around; that okay with you?"

"Yeah! Is Samantha still the head dancer?"

"Head dancer? She owns the place now! After you 'left,' she became quite the businesswoman. Owns The Gold Dragon and a half-dozen other businesses," said Michael.

"Will wonders never cease!" said James.

As the two brothers walked away from the grave, wrapped now in the wind and shadow that filled the cemetery, Michael felt the first few drops of rain.

## The End

# SKIMMING STONES

Lying flat on my stomach with my face less than a foot from the river was not the way I had planned to spend Friday night. Especially when I knew that waiting at the Shadow Creek bar, there was a martini, possibly several, with my name on it.

Not that I had a whole lot of choice in the matter. I work for the City of Tulsa as an electrical maintenance engineer, so I end up doing a lot of work in places that I would prefer not to even think about if I didn't have to; all in the name of keeping various facilities around town running.

The hours weren't the greatest, but I was pulling down decent money and didn't have to spend my days in a cubicle. This girl wasn't complaining; I'd gotten enough of that from my ex-husband, Luke; he didn't like my hours, the fact that my paycheck was bigger than his, or much of anything in our relationship. When he finally took off, three days after our first anniversary, with that dye job blonde, Denise, I couldn't have been happier.

With budget shortfalls and layoffs, my department was short-handed. Truth be told, we'd never had enough people, so making due was a way of life. That was why on a Friday night, I was in coveralls, laying on a stage floating on the Arkansas river, instead of wearing my new leather mini-skirt, boots, and suede jacket and bar hopping with my best friend, Jani.

The floating stage is anchored in a small cove. They use it for outdoor theater productions, performances by musicians, and any formal city-type ceremony that the politicians want to conduct under the open Oklahoma sky.

The problem with the place is that it was designed by an idiot. At least once a month my department got a frantic call from the stage manager saying something was wrong and it needed to be fixed, yesterday. Since Tulsa Opera was supposed to do a benefit preview at two on Sunday afternoon, the powers that be thought it would be sort of nice if things worked.

I had come out with a four-man crew around noon, then at six my boss called and told the others to go home. Less overtime, I suspect. "Look, Nancy," he had said. "You can handle it by yourself, shouldn't take you more than half an hour or so."

Yeah, right! Three hours later I was closing the last access port and breathing a long sigh of relief when I heard something hitting the side of the stage. I trailed my flashlight along the water to find see what it was. There was something I thought might be a mannequin, thrown away by frat boys at one of their drunken parties.

Okay, call me a Girl Scout, but I figured there was a chance I was wrong, so I dropped my flashlight and made a grab for whatever it was.

That took me several tries. The problem was, I couldn't get a good enough hold he dropped back into the water several times. In the process I heard the sound of coughing, that was proof enough that I wasn't trying to rescue a dummy or a corpse.

Once I did get him up on the stage I pushed his hair out of the way and discovered two important things, 'he' was a 'she, and she had my face!

Beyond a knot on the side of her head the size of a goose egg, some bruises, and a cut on her cheek, my new-found twin didn't seem to have anything wrong with her. City regulations, not to mention common sense, said I ought to call 911 or get her to the nearest hospital.

It was just that looking at that face, my face, just weirded me out so much, that I just could not see going by regulations right then as being the smartest thing in the world.

"Take it easy. You're okay. I got you out of the water," I told her.

"Where am I?" she said, her voice a cracked whisper.

"Tulsa," I said.

Don't ask me why, but right then I figured the best thing to do was get her away from there. The only place I could think of to take her was my house. I live in a suburb of Tulsa, somewhat isolated, which suited me just fine. I had been astonished when Luke had been willing to sign the place over to me as part of our divorce settlement. I took it, of course, after making sure he hadn't secretly mortgaged the place to the hilt.

Since her legs didn't seem to want to work for more than three or four steps at a time without going out from under her getting my guest inside was not easy. My cats, Paranoia and Schizo, were on the sofa but decided to take off for other places when they saw us come through the door.

Her clothes had dried some but were still smelly and wet. I managed to get one boot off of her and was just untying the other when my guest said,

"If it's seduction you have in mind, I'm afraid that you're going to be rather disappointed. I'm not feeling up for anything just now."

"Don't worry about that. I've got better ways of picking up dates than fishing them out of the river. Besides, I don't think you're my type."

"If she's not, Nancy, am I?"

Standing at the living room door was Kent Sabiani. At six-one, his lanky frame and gray-streaked goatee gave him a vaguely satanic look, which went over great with some of my more religious neighbors.

He moved so quietly that sometimes you would just look up and there he was. Kent was an Emergency Medical Technician, so I had called him on my cell phone to come give my visitor a quick once over.

"Damn it; make some noise when you come in the door!"

"Hey, I did make noise; it's not my fault that you didn't hear me. So who's your friend?"

"Name's Sian," she said in a whisper.

I saw the look on Kent's face when he got a good look at Sian. He was cool, didn't say a word, just cocked an eyebrow at me, and went to work.

I excused myself to the kitchen, where I found a couple of beers in the back of the fridge. Kent was just unwrapping a blood pressure cuff from Sian's arm when I came back. I handed him a beer.

"Thanks. Other than the obvious, bruises, scratches, and contusions, Sian seems in pretty good shape," he said. "How far did you fall?

"Don't know, but it hurt like hell," she said.

"Must have felt like hitting concrete."

 Sian nodded

"All right, that's enough," Kent said. "I would say a few hours sleep are in order.

The interrogation can wait."

The next morning I came into the kitchen and found Kent rummaging around in the cabinets, a look of frustration on his face. "So, where did you put the frying pan this time?" he asked when he saw me.

"Just for using that tone, I'm not telling you." After all, it was my kitchen and I knew where it was. "Besides, why should I help you? You left your socks and shirt hanging on the dresser mirror, again."

"Be that way and you get to cook." He grinned.

That was a good argument. I'm a decent cook, but it's nice to have someone else do the work, and I stand in awe of what Kent can do in a kitchen. "Cabinet! Just to the right of the stove!" I said quickly.

Kent pulled the skillet out, and fetched eggs, milk, and a variety of other things from the refrigerator. I've never been able to figure out if he has specific recipes or just works with what's there. The results speak for themselves.

"Is there anything I can do to help?"

Sian walked into the kitchen wearing my heavy red bathrobe. A shower and some sleep seemed to have done her a world of good. The bruises were still prominent, but in the light of day looked like they would heal. She moved a bit stiffly, favoring her right leg, but, given the circumstances that was understandable.

"Just grab a stool," I said. "Kent is working his magic."

"A moment later he presented us each with a tall glass of orange juice. The odor of blueberry muffins began to fill the kitchen, followed a few minutes later by Kent setting a plate of them in front of Sian and me. He turned his attention back to the stove. I knew omelets would soon follow.

"Okay," I said. "So, feel like answering a few questions?"

"Ask away," Sian said, slicing a muffin and layering butter onto it. "This is very good. She was right when she called it magic."

"Thank you. So, what happened?" Kent said, without turning around.

"You wouldn't believe that I just got a little bit plastered and fell into the river?" I just arched an eyebrow at her and didn't say a thing. "Well, I didn't think so, especially if you've looked in the mirror anytime. The long and the short of it is, I'm you."

"Really?"

Sian nodded as she took a sip from her glass.

"If you were able to run a DNA test on the two of us you'd see that we are genetically the same person. Only I'm not from this world."

"Unless you were cloned by aliens, or are a part of some sort of secret government conspiracy, that leaves only two possible explanations," said Kent. "Time travel or parallel world?"

Sian looked at him, shocked. "I'm impressed. You keeping him around on a long-term basis?" she asked me.

I didn't answer. Instead, I reached across the counter and grabbed Sian's left arm, pushing back the sleeve. Midway up the arm was a formation of veins, making the letter H, clearly visible beneath her skin. A jagged scar, about four inches in length, bisected it. I bared my arm to show an identical mark but reversed. I'd definitely call this a bit more than circumstantial evidence.

"I am from a parallel world," she said. "Where history, as you know it, ran differently, because of different choices."

"So how did you end up in our corner of the time-space continuum?" asked Kent.

"To make a long story short, I'm a runaway princess." Kent had to struggle to keep from laughing, this was beginning to sound like something out of those fantasy novels he's so fond of reading.

"Let me see if I have this straight," I said. "You're me, from a parallel world, where you're a princess. But you decided to take it on the lam from your life as one of the royals and came here."

"Not at first. I left just over a year ago. I've probably been in seven or eight different worlds before this one."

Sian made a gesture in the air and a small globe of light appeared just above the palm of her hand. It hovered there for a moment and was gone.

"Kent isn't the only one who can do magic. It looks like magic, but there are sound principles of science behind it," she said. "Problem is that is about all I can do."

"A handy talent. So why did you leave home?" Kent asked.

Sian laid the remnants of her muffin down on a napkin. "They wanted to make me Queen."

"Queen?" I said. "I don't think you have any glass ceiling where you come from."

She cocked an eyebrow at me but went on. "My Daddy had decided it was time for him to have a co-ruler; someone who would do most of the work while he took it easy. I may be the eldest, but my brother is far more suited to the throne. When he wouldn't let me abdicate I faked my death and ran. The problem was he didn't believe it. He commissioned the Guild of Head Hunters to find me and bring me home. They've come close too many times."

"You figured to hide from them here in Tulsa?" Kent asked.

"Actually, no," she sighed. "I left a trail for the Head Hunters to follow, I had planned to lay a trap for them and then permanently lose them in the desert."

Permanently lose? To me, that said kill them and dump the bodies.

"So, why are you in Tulsa?" asked Kent.

"Because of her," Sian pointed at me. "For reasons that I don't understand whenever I enter a new world, I tend to end up close to myself, if I'm still alive in that world. There have been a few where I was dead or had never been born."

"I bet that was a fun discovery," I said.

Kent picked up a muffin from the tin and began to gingerly peel the paper cup from around it.

"Sian, one thing that you haven't mentioned is just how you're able to go hopping from parallel world to parallel world. So what went wrong?" I asked.

"What makes you think anything went wrong?"

"A thirty-foot drop into the river sort of suggests that things didn't work the way you planned them to work."

Sian laughed. "Oh, they didn't work the way I had planned them. Travel between the worlds is a combination of making your mind perceive things differently and then stepping through the gate. Ideally, you need a set of rune stones to open that gate. I grabbed some of the best before I left home

"The only trouble is that I lost my rune stones. My father's chief warlock taught me ways of duplicating the rune door with my mind, using a variety of herbs, native flora, and pharmaceuticals. The problem is the last two worlds haven't had what I needed and I had to use substitutes. They didn't always work right."

"So you're saying, when you do this you're on drugs," Kent grinned. "Talk about your ultimate bad acid trip. So if you don't know where you are, does this mean that those Head Hunters of yours won't be able to find you?"

Sian stared at the counter for a long time. "I can only hope so."

"Well, I never had a sister, so you're about the closest I'm going to come to one," I said, putting my arm around her shoulder. "You're welcome to stay here for as long a visit as you want."

If she was going to stay around, Sian was going to need "a life", at least on paper. Kent just said to leave it to him. He knew a hacker who could do the job.

"Is this guy good?" I asked.

"Oh, yeah," he grinned. "The guy I have in mind is the one who teaches the CIA forgery department how to do things."

That done it was time to do something else, just as important. I looked at Sian's clothes we'd left in the laundry room. They were not in good shape. She was going to need more than what I had found her in, and more than just borrowed things from my closet. Time to go shopping.

We hit the local mall and found everything Sian would need, not to mention some neat things for myself. Just after noon, I decided it was time to introduce Sian to native dishes, i.e.: pizza. Meals in hand, we found a table near the stage at the center of the food court.

There were a bunch of guys there, dressed in combat fatigues, faces painted in camouflage paint all holding weird-looking metal guns. The weapons looked like the sort of things my cousins Tim and Randy had played with when we were growing up, not practical looking but the sort of thing that thrills a twelve-year-old male.

When they began showing off some round balls and inserting them in the guns it dawned on me that these weren't real army types, but paintball gamers.

I explained the concept to Sian and she just shook her head. "They do this for fun?"

I was about to turn my attention back to a slice of pizza when I looked toward the restrooms. The air in front of them had begun to shimmer and fold in on itself. Then someone was standing there. He was big, six-four at least, wearing a dark floppy hat and a leather jacket.

"Slowly look over toward the restrooms," I told Sian. "I think we have a visitor."

"I don't have to," Sian was staring at the shiny metal wall of the Chinese fast food place. She could see a slightly blurry version of this fellow without a problem.

"A Head Hunter? Does he know you're here?" I said, softy.

"Remember what I said about being drawn to this area because you were here. Look up on the stage." She pointed at a man standing at the back of the group of camo-dressed performers. He was shaggier and maybe didn't weigh as much, but I could see the resemblance.

I was about to suggest that we ease our way out of there when things began to go a bit haywire. One of the paintball guys tripped over something, his own feet probably, gun in hand, and almost fell. One thing he did do was accidentally squeeze off a shot that went straight out into the audience and hit the Head Hunter square on the chest. I can imagine where he would have hit if there had been time to aim.

The Head Hunter looked down, and touched the fresh paint with one finger. "I just had that cleaned!" he said and headed for the stage.

Not being your shy retiring type, Sian grabbed one of the metal chairs that filled the food court. As the Head Hunter passed she brought it down hard across the man's back. That proved effective enough to put him on the floor, surprise is the best weapon. A quick grab under his shirt and she jerked something loose.

"Let's go!" she said.

We made it to the car and I hit the gas. How we got out of there without being stopped did it I still don't know.

"Damn, damn, damn," she muttered as I pointed the car toward the street.

"What was that you got from him?" I asked.

"These," she opened the small leather back and poured out a half dozen flat stones, each one of the carved with an intricate rune.

Sian spread the runestones out on my dining room table. There were six, none bigger than a quarter. All were slick and cool to the touch.

"This isn't good. If one of them found their way here, that means the others know where he went. So if he doesn't report back, and he can't without these, then they will come looking for him." she said.

"Then why did you take them?" I asked. "I know, I know, it seemed the thing to do at the time. Can we just smash them and hope the others don't show up on our doorstep?" I got my answer with just the look in Sian's eyes.

Smashing those pebbles would be a very last resort.

"How long will it be before the other show up?" asked Kent.

"If I've read these alignments correctly," she nodded. "I should judge sometime late tonight, give or take a couple of hours. They are going to try for an area along the river, probably somewhere north of where I arrived, something solid I would expect. They can't walk on water any more than I could."

"Good, then maybe it's time for you to stop running," said Kent.

"I'm not going back!" protested Sian.

"You don't have to if we work this right." The look on Kent's face suggested that he had something in mind. "It strikes me that there is a fairly simple answer to your problems, in my never-to-be-humble opinion."

"Oh, really?" asked Sian.

"Sure, we're just going to have to kill you."

Standing, at two a.m. on an abandoned bridge a mile north of the floating stage, with a strong northeasterly breeze blowing off the river, I was not what you would describe as a happy camper. More like an irritated, cold and angry camper. I didn't think that Sian or Kent were any more comfortable right then than I was. When Kent had breezed back in late that afternoon he was carrying half-a-dozen large boxes. "Have a look at these," he said. "I think you'll find them interesting."

Interesting was a good word. I was wearing the contents of several of them: a one-piece black leather catsuit, covered in chains and metal studs that were so tight I could barely breathe. Sian had to help me get into the thing and get everything zipped. Even the ankle-length duster didn't do a thing to keep me warm, though it did provide a place to keep a loaded Beretta and a fully charged Taser.

If Sian had read those stones correctly, this was where the Head Hunters were supposed to show up. That was a big if to my way of thinking. Of course, we might get lucky, have them miss, and end up drowning in the middle of the river. I wasn't counting on that.

Frankly, I was about ready to give up this idea and revert to Plan B, once we came up with Plan B when something happened to the air about twenty feet off to my left. I motioned for Sian and Kent to stay hidden.

The air seemed to waver for a moment, fold in on itself, and then there were two men standing in the center of the bridge. After our first Head Hunter, I think I expected some sort of cross between a barbarian and a biker. That wasn't what we got; more like a matching pair of lawyer boys, one was scarecrow-thin with a smile that seemed to take up three-fourths of his face, and the other was short, bald, and looked like one of my cats could take him two falls out of three.

"I think this may be the place we're looking for. It feels right," the tall one said.

"I hope so, it's about time our luck changed," his companion said.

That was my cue. I pushed the duster back and strode forward. "All right, you two scumballs. This time you are completely out of luck. You're mine!" Hey, even if I was cold and scared out of my wits, I think I presented a fairly fierce picture right then.

Seeing me, they just stood staring for several seconds. That was enough time for Kent to come over the side of the bridge, where he had been perched, and clobber one of them with a blackjack. I enjoyed very much using the Taser on the other. Once they were down, I made sure they were still breathing, then we hog-tied them; feet and hands together behind

The air seemed to waver for a moment...

their backs, with nooses around their necks.

"I guess this is place for Act Two," I said as Kent waved capsules of smelling salts under their noses.

They jerked awake and it didn't take them too long to figure out that they were in trouble. The smaller one looked around and started to speak, but thought better of it. The other one just stared at me, his face impassive and waiting.

"Good evening, boys. So, do the two of you have names of any sort?"

"Aye, m'lady," the taller one said, pronouncing each word carefully. "I'm Carson Sal'se and he's Vernon Myth'rn. If we have offended you or broken any local laws we do most humbly apologize."

"Well, isn't that just too, too cute. You've made a serious mistake, showing up on my lands, just when I'm in a very, very bad mood!" I said.

I began to pace back and forth. In the distance, I could see the lights of the 21st street traffic bridge, flanked by the expressway bridge fifty yards beyond that. I couldn't help but grin at the idea of how the passing drivers might react to this scene. Of course, explaining this whole scene to any police officers who showed up might be more than a bit difficult.

"The treasury is a little low right now and the price of two prime slaves like you two would certainly help fatten it up. I understand that there is a shortage of workers in the okra fields to the south. They'll be here shortly, for my little package over there. You fellows wouldn't happen to be with her, now would you?"

It wasn't easy for either of the Head Hunters to see where I had pointed, but they tried. One of Kent's other boxes had contained a filmy affair of white silk and transparent gossamer fabric.

Wrapped around Sian it looked as exotic, in its way, as what I had on. It made what I had on look warm and comfortable. Kent dragged her forward to stand closer to the rest of us. Sian was blindfolded and her hands bound behind her.

"It's her! I told you we would find her!" said Myth'rn. He tried to get to his feet but got no more than a couple of inches when the rope around his neck choked him off.

"You dared to violate my territory for that?"

"Yes, m'lady. She is to become a queen in her own right."

I began to laugh. "I doubt that she will be good for anything like that, not now anyway. This wench showed up here three days ago, tried to take me in a fight, and lost. Instead of killing her, I had her dosed with a drug that I use a good deal in my business. The stuff helps new slaves adjust to life in the bawdy houses I operate. That is if I don't decide just to get rid of her like I'm thinking of getting rid of you two." I knew one thing; I had to keep them more than a bit uncertain of just what was going on, before they started asking too many questions, like how we happened to be there and just where they were going to show up.

The look on the faces of the two Head Hunters was something akin to grief and shock, with a healthy dose of fear thrown in for good measure.

"This wasn't how you had wanted things to work out?" I asked.

"No, m'lady. Our guild accepted the commission to return her to the throne. It's obvious now; we have failed," he said." When we return we will be in disgrace."

"If I allow you to return. Maybe I should just feed you to the fishes. Can either of you swim?"

"Swim? N...no, m'lady."

"You two are such pains. But then so is she, and I'm not in the mood." I pulled out the Taser and jammed it against Sian's neck. The effect was quick and certain, she jerked like a marionette whose strings had been dropped, then crumpled to the ground. She lay there, eyes open and empty, her tongue hanging limply from her mouth.

"We'll just compost what's left of her," I said.

I let my words digest with them for several moments as their eyes darted between me and Sian's still form. Then I reached over and pulled their shirts open, just as Sian had told me to expect, two identical leather bags were hanging around their necks. I yanked them free.

"I was going to kill you, and dump you over the bridge, but the river's too polluted as is," I said. "I have a better idea."

I gestured for Kent. He grabbed the shoulders of the smaller man and I grabbed his feet. We rolled him on top of the other one, face to face. I shoved one rune stone each between their lips.

"Don't swallow fellows," I laughed. "You've got one chance, scum. I'd advise you to take it."

They understood what I was talking about, leaned forward, and touched the stones together. The air shivered, folded in on itself and the two Head Hunters were gone.

"That's one way to make an exit," Kent said.

Sian moaned and began to blink her eyes. Kent scrambled to her side, checking her vitals. "Did it work?" she managed to ask.

"You betcha, sis," I said. "I have a feeling they're going to be required to think very fast to explain what happened. In fact, I'm fairly sure they won't be able to admit a thing about what really happened. As far as your father is concerned you are gone and will not be returning anytime soon."

"That's good; I just wish it didn't have to be this way. I love Daddy, but he can be hard-headed," she said. "Oh, but that thing you hit me with, sister mine, hurt like you wouldn't believe. Look, before we go much further, would somebody mind untying me? And I would appreciate a coat of some kind. It's cold out here."

Kent took a knife and cut the ropes around Sian's wrists, helping her stand up in the process. "We need to have a long talk, Kent, about your taste in women's clothes," she said. I didn't have to look over there to know he was putting on his totally innocent "I don't know what you're talking about face just then.

I had to say it had been an interesting weekend. I reached into my pocket and touched the rune stones. It occurred to me that smooth and flat as they were they would be perfect for skimming. I wondered how far I could throw them.

"No, maybe another time," I said to the wind.

"I don't know about you two, but I could do with some hot coffee," said Kent

"What's coffee?" asked Sian.

## **The End**

# WHERE THE SHADOWS BEGAN

Paris, 1910

Inspector John Raymond Legrasse leaned back and listened to the steady thump of the train wheels as they rolled over the tracks. The sound had long since faded into the background for him. The sound was still there, just somewhere *else*, and that was exactly where he wanted it.

Legrasse had never particularly been that fond of train travel; he just accepted it as something that you had to do if you were going to get from one place to another in any reasonable amount of time. It wasn't as if there were that many stagecoaches running anymore, and, while Legrasse could drive, he hadn't yet taken the plunge and purchased an automobile.

"Not that it could have gotten me here," he mused softly. Being able to drive from New Orleans, in the United States, to Paris, France, would have been a quite remarkable trick, worthy of the pen of Verne or Wells, or something that had come out of Edison's idea factory in Menlo Park.

"Excuse me, sir. Is that seat taken?"

Legrasse opened one eye and looked up. The speaker was a tall grey-haired man dressed in a dark suit. He was pointing at the high-backed chair, one of the dozen that filled the smoking compartment, across from where Legrasse was sitting, "No, no. Feel free."

He carefully extracted one, cut the end with a pen knife, and struck a match to it, holding the flame close until the end was glowing red.

"Would you care for one?" the stranger asked, shaking out another long brown tube from his case. "Hand rolled, Cuban, made for me in a little shop in Havana."

Legrasse actually preferred his pipe but had been known to indulge in a good cigar every now and then.

"There is something familiar about you," said the policeman.

"I was wondering when you would recognize me, although it has been almost five years since I was in New Orleans and our paths crossed," chuckled the gray-haired man. "Ardan, Michel Ardan, a pleasure to see you again, Inspector."

"Yes, you were the fellow that the War Department brought in, from the

Baltimore Gun Club when the New Orleans armory was broken into. They were rather insistent that we drop everything and deal with it."

"Indeed. I'm semi-retired now, but still do some consulting for the War Department," said Ardan. "And yourself?"

Legrasse chuckled. "I, sir, am "on holiday", not by choice. My superiors felt that it was a good idea that I take some time off to reestablish my health after a recent investigation."

The chief of police himself had taken Legrasse aside and explained that the inspector *would* be taking some time away from New Orleans, with pay, of course, if he wanted to be able to return to his job. There had been a matter of some political toes that had been stepped on during the investigation and the chief felt it was prudent for Legrasse to absent himself until things had been smoothed over.

"My grandmother recently passed, at the age of 90, and I discovered that I was the heir to some small properties here in France. She had not been back since the time of the '48 revolution and I was her only living relative. This seemed as good a time as any to make the trip."

Legrasse had told that story several times during his trip and almost believed it himself.

"I hope you will allow yourself time to see some of the sights of Paris," said Ardan. "It is a one-of-a-kind city."

Legrasse glanced down at the issue of the *Echo de France* that he had been reading earlier, at the three-inch square advertisement announcing a performance by the Hastur Company. The ad was dominated by a yellow face mask.

"I may take in a play or two. I've always had a fondness for the theatre," he said.

Legrasse pulled his overcoat tighter, blocking out the wind as best he could, and looked around at the buildings, most of them sealed with weather-scored planks hammered across windows and doors. There were a few ancient business signs on some of the buildings, but most were bare of even a street number. The whole place had an air of decay, even in the middle of the day.

Legrasse turned suddenly at the sound of a clattering of wheels behind him. His hand automatically reached into the pocket of his greatcoat to close around the butt of the well-oiled revolver that had accompanied him from America. His fingers relaxed their grip when he saw that it was a large brown delivery wagon, pulled by two dapple gray horses. He watched them until they turned off to the left and vanished from sight.

That was when he noticed the other building, just down the street. It had once been a theater, though the name was long since gone from what he suspected had been a marquee sticking out over the street. Not one of the big glittering palaces like the behemoth Paris Opera, even if the place was reported to be haunted, or the Follies-Bergere, and the Varieties, but a smaller, more intimate place.

Legrasse had seen too many buildings like this back home in New Orleans, places that had long since been lost to the city and now clung by only the tiniest thread to existence. Everything about the theatre said its time had long since passed.

Crossing the street, Legrasse could feel the wind die away as he got closer to the building. The air was still and felt almost like a living thing that had taken a deep breath and was holding it.

He pushed at it, expecting nothing to happen. Instead, it moved, just enough to let him know that it was not locked. Legrasse allowed time for his eyes to adjust to the darkness before stepping across the threshold.

A heavy layer of dust on the floor showed that no one had been there in a very long time on the wall broken gas jets hung at odd angles across torn and heavily water-stained wallpaper.

At the far end of the hallway were twin doors with the word auditorium painted over them. A glance inside showed him tiered seating on risers that, given the size of the room, would not have seated more than fifty or so. Many of them were broken and overturned. The walls looked like they had been painted black, though the color merged so much with the darkness of the room that it was difficult to tell where the shadows began and the walls ended.

As he looked back at the front door of the theater, he noticed that there was something there; something that he would have sworn was not there when he had come inside. It was a flyer, held in place by small tack nails at each corner, the kind that were spread all over the city announcing various events; plastered up by hordes of street urchins to earn a few coins to fill their stomachs with.

Pulling it off the wall, Legrasse stepped outside, letting the daylight illuminate the paper. It featured a face mask, colored an oddly sick-looking yellow, in the center of the page. The wording was in French but it appeared to announce a one-time-only performance of a play called Le Roi en Jaune——"The King in Yellow", billed as one of the most dangerous theatrical creations in decades, being produced under the auspices of the Hastur Company.

The performance was set in the very building where he stood.

"I have to admit that I had another reason for coming to Paris, besides looking up my family properties," said Legrasse. The police inspector had always prided himself on being a good judge of people, often going with his gut feeling on a situation even if the facts contradicted it. So while there were things he would have liked to know about Michael Ardan, given their joint experience five years before Legrasse felt he could be trusted.

"So what is it that brings you to Paris?" Ardan asked as he and the police inspector sat down for drinks and dinner at Legrasse's hotel.

"Two years ago there was a massacre in a local theater in New Orleans, forty people dead, literally ripped to shreds, blood was everywhere and nary a clue as to who did it or what their motive was. I've been a policeman for a long time and am no stranger to murder, but there was something wrong with what we found in that theater; something that made it feel as if the very substance of those poor people had been sucked out of them," Legrasse said. "Like marrow from a bone. Two of the policemen who had investigated the scene with me died shortly thereafter, one by drowning and one by blowing his head off with a shotgun on the front steps of city hall."

Ardan nodded and took a drink before speaking. "How many of the dead were audience members and how many were actors?" he asked.

"As best could be determined they were all audience members. There was no sign of the actors or any member of the production company, and we could find no trace of them in New Orleans. The Hastur Company seemed to have vanished from the face of the earth until four months ago.

"I was in the middle of investigating a drug smuggling operation when we arrested the man behind it. I found a flyer among his papers. It was an announcement of a production of 'The King in Yellow by the Hastur Company, a single performance, set for Paris, tomorrow night."

"Interesting," said Ardan. "Especially given the conditions you described of that theater. I have a feeling that there is something you haven't mentioned about why you are here."

"While I did twist a few political noses during the investigation, I considered it a stroke of luck that the chief suggested I take an extended holiday. It's true that I don't take kindly to people being killed like that in New Orleans."

Legrasse produced an envelope from his pocket and handed it across the table to Ardan. Inside was a small piece of high-grade white paper. Embossed on it were the words 'The King in Yellow,' followed by a Bourbon Street address in New Orleans and the name Inspector John Raymond Legrasse.

"It appears you were on the invitation list," said Ardan.

"And I probably would have been there had I not injured my ankle the night before."

Ardan nodded and said nothing for several minutes. "I have some contacts in the local theatrical community, not to mention a few more esoteric places. I can make a few inquiries, then I think that you and I shall go to the theatre."

"I appreciate the help. I'm a bit far from my usual sources of information and, while I can make myself understood in it, French and I are not always on the best of terms. There is no need, though, for you to put yourself in harm's way," said Legrasse.

Truth was, he wasn't all that confident in his mind of what was going on, only that it was something that he could not let go of until there were some kinds of answers.

"Nonsense, you have piqued my curiosity." the older man said.

Legrasse remembered that phrase several hours later as he sat alone in the hotel bar. Ardan had departed sometime before, but Legrasse knew that if he had sought sleep it would not come. He had been nursing a glass of bourbon for half an hour listening to the music played by a quartet at the far end of the room.

"Are you as bored by this miserable excuse for music as I am?" The woman in front of Legrasse wore a provocative gown of green with a dash of black and a single emerald choker around her throat. She was tall and angular, her emerald eyes looking at him in a way that Legrasse could feel through and through.

"I never claimed to be a music critic."

"Music should be able to take the listener and carry him to other places, places that were or could be or perhaps should never be," she said. Legrasse had the feeling that those last words were not directed at him. He wasn't all that sure he wanted to know whom they were meant for.

"Perhaps," he said slowly. "Though one can never be sure until the musicians begin to play what the piece will do."

"Indeed. How do you feel about music and the theatre?"

"It can be interesting, if well done, painful if not."

Without asking permission the woman took the chair that Ardan had occupied earlier. For a long moment neither spoke, listening to the music instead. When the musicians shifted into a different tune, one that sounded vaguely familiar, something changed.

"I can't help but say that piece comes close to fitting the description of painful," she said.

"You may be right," he smiled. "I don't believe we've been introduced, madam."

"We haven't. You may call me Cassilda. Should I call you John or Raymond, Inspector?"

Legrasse's eyes darted over the room, scanning the few others in the bar for any sign that they might be in league with her. She was enticing, a mystery wrapped up in an enigma, the answer to which would probably be as mundane as anything.

"Perhaps we should keep it formal and you call me Inspector. Only my late grandmother called me Raymond and I don't know you well enough to suggest my first name as an alternative."

From her handbag, the woman drew two small pieces of cardboard. She slid them across the table toward Legrasse, holding them in place in front of him with the edge of her fingernail, the red polish glowed for a moment, then faded to a darker shade close to that of blood.

"I've brought you something, sir. Something that you will find far more entertaining than this pitiful excuse for music that is currently assaulting our ears could ever hope to be."

Inspector John Raymond Legrasse drew a long breath and continued to stare at the woman. His eyes barely registered what she had placed on the table.

Very deliberately Legrasse reached across the table and laid his forefinger on the pieces of cardboard, carefully not touching Cassilda. He drew them toward him, turning them over. They were tickets, emblazoned with an eyeless yellow mask, and the words 'The Hastur Company presents for one night only The King in Yellow' worked into the design that ran up and down the side. Across the end they read "Doors open at 7:30, no one will be admitted after the performance begins."

Legrasse felt a chill as he stared at the tickets, he could feel the weight of the other invitation in his coat pocket.

"So, are you interested?" Cassilda said, her voice a low sound that outweighed any other noise in the room.

"For me? How kind, since there is more than one I wonder if you were planning on accompanying me?"

"That would be difficult since I must be on stage. Though afterwards, who can say."

With that, Cassilda rose and walked toward the far door, her figure cutting its way along the shadowed portico. At the last moment, she turned and said something. Legrasse had the impression that she was speaking to him, though he could not distinguish the words.

. "No one seems to know anything about this Hastur Company, not even any rumors of the spicy and salacious variety, and for actors not to know that kind of gossip is damned unusual," related Ardan. "I even contacted the Diogenes Club in London and they professed to know nothing about the Hastur Company. The play's been around for a long time and there are rumors about it that are fairly bizarre."

"So I guess we have to go in there cold and see what happens," said Legrasse.

"So, tell me more about this young woman, Cassilda did you say her name was?"

"That's what she claimed. I tried to follow her but I lost sight of her in the street outside of the hotel. It seems like her main objective was to deliver the tickets, so I'm getting the feeling that we are *expected*."

"Shall we be off? After all, we wouldn't want to miss the curtain, now would we?" Ardan replied.

Two cabs had refused their fare when told the address, forcing Legrasse and Ardan to walk. As they moved along the streets, the lights of Paris began to flicker into existence around the two men.

As they walked, Legrasse could not shake the feeling that they were being followed. Yet he could not spot who the watchers might be. He just felt in his gut that they were there, watching and making sure that the two men found their way to their final destination.

"I regret that I am the only one of us who is armed," Legrasse admitted as they neared the theater.

"Whatever gave you that idea," Ardan held up his walking stick so Legrasse could see the heavy metal ball that was at the end, and then he opened his coat to reveal a rather formidable-looking pistol holstered under his shoulder. "I do work for the Gun Club, after all. I've traveled all over the United States, as well as the world, from Opar to Shangri-La and Maple White Land. So I long ago learned the value of having weapons to hand."

Legrasse allowed himself to smile. Things were looking up, at least for a moment. He did wonder how long that feeling would last.

Things can change in a short time, that much Legrasse knew, but as he and his companion turned the corner onto the same street he had stood on less than a day before, he found himself amazed at what confronted him.

Most of the buildings were still dark and abandoned-looking. Only the theatre had changed. What had been a wreck now looked as new as the first day it had opened for business; the doors were illuminated with gold filigree and the façade had a feel of opulent decadence about it. A small group, dressed in tuxedos and gowns, stood in front of the theater waiting for their chance to enter this dream palace.

"This hardly matches your description of this place," said Ardan. "I must say, these people seem to be on their toes when it comes to remodeling."

"Tell me something I don't know," said Legrasse.

"I'm pleased to see that you decided to come, Inspector," greeted Cassilda. The woman had come out through a smaller door just to one side of the main entrance. She wore a yellow gown draped in the classic Greek style, a thin silver headband holding her hair in place.

"How could I refuse a suggestion from so lovely a lady."

"Then let me not keep you from '*The King*'." She gestured for them to follow her.

Once inside, Cassilda pointed toward a curtain that led out into the main hallway. Like the outside, the inside of the theater had been reborn, in lush colors and gilded accouterments. A feeling of ultimate hedonism seemed to permeate everything, even the air itself.

"Bruno will show you to your seats," Cassilda smiled at Legrasse before she disappeared down a hallway that he guessed gave the performers access to the backstage area.

Bruno proved to be a medium-sized man with the palest face that Legrasse had seen this side of a corpse who had been floating in the swamp for a week. Yet there was a spark of yellow in his eyes that reminded him of a sputtering candle fighting to stay lit. He wore a tuxedo that looked as if it had been made for someone several inches taller and many pounds heavier than he.

"You are Cassilda's guests," Bruno said after Legrasse handed him the tickets.

Most of the seats in the theatre were posh red leather creations, inlaid with designs similar to what bracketed the building's front door. Here and there among the fifty or so seats were four or five, mixed in among the rest that were also red, but a darker, harsher red.

"The performance will begin shortly," said Bruno.

The people that they had seen outside began to make their way into the auditorium; most were talking in the way of theatre patrons through the ages about dinner, their lives, and their thoughts on the coming play. From the few words here and there, broken sentences and half-heard statements it was obvious that no one had much of an idea just what 'The King in Yellow' might be about, only that it was infamous and attending the exclusive performance was a social coup.

Gradually the gas lamps on the wall flickered to life, growing slowly brighter. When the stage was illuminated, Bruno stepped through the curtain. He had discarded his ill-fitting tuxedo for an imperial Roman toga that seemed to have been designed especially for him.

"Ladies and Gentlemen, I bid you welcome to this performance of 'The King in Yellow,'" he said, his voice booming out into the small room. "This play is one of the most banned in the world. I cannot count the number of cities and countries which have proclaimed that its words cannot be performed within their borders. There are those who say that when he had finished writing it, the playwright cut his own throat with the very quill that he used to pen it. Perhaps this is a warning, offering you a chance to depart, or perhaps it is nothing more than empty words, building up our performance this evening."

An uneven wave of laughter filled the room, slowly shifting over to applause.

Bruno spoke slowly, a grin breaking his passive face. "Very well, you have made your choice, so let me say simply, on with the show."

"Ladies and gentlemen, I bid you welcome..."

The light shifted, casting a mixture of lights, yellow, red, and white, across the stage. A cowled and caped figure came onto the stage, head bowed, face turned from the audience, and moved across until it stood on the edge only a foot from the people who sat on the front row. Two additional figures, each nearly identical to the first emerged, taking up positions to form a curved line just a hand's breadth from the audience. Each of them wore identical full face masks, all three a pale, sickening yellow.

Legrasse exhaled, he realized that he had been holding his breath since Bruno had finished speaking. As much as he wanted to, he could not look away from the stage.

Something nagged at him as he watched, even more so than when he and Ardan had entered the theater.

Music came from somewhere in the wings on stage left, a harpsichord or a piano of some kind; in the distance, other instruments echoed, a drum and a flute vibrating like a heartbeat.

On some level, Legrasse was aware of the play as it moved through scene after scene, but from one moment to the next he could not have recounted what had just happened on the stage. It was in the second act that Cassilda spoke to the man who had been designated the King.

"Along the shore the cloud wave breaks. ..." the rest of the words merged into an indistinguishable din. Yet he could hear another voice, one growing stronger and louder with each word that it spoke.

Bruno came through the door at the side of the auditorium, followed by a figure wrapped head to toe in a bright yellow robe, its face also wearing a yellow mask identical to the ones that the first performers had worn. The two were shrouded in the light from the hallway, then merged with the shadows as the door swung shut behind them.

Whoever this was had a thick leather-bound book that he carried in both his hands, holding it in front of him like a sacred chalice being brought to the alter.

"Hail! The true King in Yellow is among us," chanted Bruno.

Legrasse nudged Ardan and pointed toward the newcomers. The other man turned his head one way and then another as if he were having trouble focusing on the figures.

"Is it....." said Ardan.

"I don't know," said Legrasse. Around the tiny auditorium, the other audience members had begun to sway, chanting the same words over and over. Clothes began to fly off and moans replaced words as arms and flesh merged in syncopation with the chant.

Legrasse felt a woman's hands moving over him from behind, her body plastered hard against him; Legrasse found himself staring into the eyes of Cassilda.

"Come to me, John. Now is the time, the time that I have been waiting for. I need you; I want you; I have to have you as part of me and mine. I reached for you in New Orleans, but you did not respond."

Around them, a cornucopia of sounds, flesh against flesh, voices moaning at an animal level, filled Legrasse's ears. He found himself struggling to not lose himself in them, to not surrender to what they promised.

"What are you?" he demanded.

"More than you could conceive, not even in your wildest yearnings or nightmares."

Legrasse twisted to one side, pulling back from her. The elegant gown that enwrapped Cassilda earlier was now torn and marked with splotches. He thought he could smell...something, an odor that turned his stomach. Just then his hand brushed against the butt of his gun, it was like touching the ends of an electric wire, the pain something that he could grab onto and hold, something real something that he could understand.

It took him two tries before he could close his fingers around the gun. Once it was free he slammed the gun hard against the side of Cassilda's face. The impact was a satisfying sound.

Cassilda flew to the side, slamming into Ardan and knocking the other man backward across the theatre seat to his side. That seemed enough to drag him out of the trance that had enwrapped the audience for 'The King in Yellow.'

All around Legrasse and Ardan the sounds of moans and body against body had changed. Now there were screams; pain and terror mixed into a new unholy sound that echoed off the walls. People were ripping each other apart, the gaslights on the wall flaring like a heartbeat to illuminate the scene.

Over the whole thing, The King in Yellow presided, chanting, Bruno holding the huge leather-bound volume open in front of him. With each passing second the book seemed to grow bigger, as one after another the audience members were ripped apart.

"I would say the time has come to make an ungraceful exit, my friend," Ardan said as he kicked at Cassilda who was crawling along the floor toward him, laughing maniacally.

"I couldn't agree more," Legrasse said as he fired twice toward The King. If the bullets struck the figure, Legrasse couldn't tell' the figure seemed absorbed by the book and the chant that came from beneath his mask.

Then it came to Legrasse. "The book," he shouted to Ardan. The other man seemed puzzled at first, but then understanding washed over his face. Both men began to fire. One of their shots struck Bruno, whose grin did not fade as he collapsed in a heap on the floor. But a few shots struck home, and the effect was almost immediate; everything around them, people, colors, chairs, walls, the very light itself seemed to merge into one, spinning around and around. Legrasse felt his stomach go out from underneath him. It was only by some miracle that he managed to stay on his feet.

And then they were on the street. Legrasse had no memory of leaving the theater, he was simply one place and a heartbeat later he was somewhere else.

The theater was gone, or, rather, abandoned again, the boards once again blocked the doors, and layer upon layer of Paris grime blackened the windows.

Legrasse looked at his companion.

"Don't ask me, I don't know," said Ardan.

Neither did Legrasse, and he had the feeling in the pit of his stomach that he probably would never know, and that was a good thing.

A ripped flyer rolled past in the wind. Legrasse couldn't be sure but he thought he saw the image of a yellow mask and the words 'The Hastur Company presents' on it.

New York City, 1925

"Belknapius, would you be so good as to have a look at this?"

Howard Lovecraft gestured at the wooden fence where layer after layer of advertising posters had been pasted. The particular poster that had caught his attention was half covered by another in the endless chain of advertising that adorned virtually any fence or empty wall in any of the five boroughs of New York."

"What is it, Howard?" Howard was a walking example of the word eccentric, from referring to himself as Grandpa or the Old Gentleman to concocted nicknames for friends and correspondents like calling Frank by a Latinized version of his middle name Belknap.

The two of them made quite a pair. Howard's long frame, which seemed to have grown leaner in the past several months, contrasted with Frank's shorter stature, neatly trimmed mustache, and thick glasses. Since Lovecraft's relocation to New York from his beloved Providence, the two of them had spent many hours roaming the streets of Brooklyn.

"It's this poster," said Lovecraft. "It presents a bit of a surprise for this Babylonian berg. An acting company is presenting a bit of theatre with an unusual name.

That does not suggest the sort of material that you would see on the so-called Great White Way, or that might be scored by those hacks on Tin Pan Alley."

The shorter man scratched his chin; it amazed him that his friend knew anything about live theatre, let alone musical theatre. The poster showed a full face mask, vaguely resembling one of the traditional drama masks, only this was the oddest shade of yellow.

"And what is it? Some lost Shakespeare play perhaps, or a revival of "Our American Cousin?'"

"' The King in Yellow'," said the tall man.

"Never heard of it," his companion replied. "I can't read all of the poster; too much of the thing is covered over, but it looks like there is only going to be one performance, which, if I understand theatre, is most unusual. Besides, I didn't think you were interested in theatre."

"Sonia has been trying to bring it to my attention. My dear wife wants to widen my horizons. Unfortunately, the date is Saturday next and I am otherwise obligated. Perhaps you could go and report back."

"Saturday, no," said Frank. "My parents and I are going to Maryland to visit some distant cousins of ours."

The long lean man let out a sigh. "I must say the few moments of culture that this town manages to bring forth are just as quickly gone."

"I shouldn't worry about it, Howard. Plays come and go and then come back again and again. Sometimes it seems like there is no way to stop one if it is popular. Look, let me stand you to an ice cream soda."

"A capitol idea, Belknapius, a capitol idea" said Howard. As the two men walked away, the wind whipped up and ripped another piece of the poster from the wall, leaving only the image of the yellow mask behind it.

## The End

# SEASON FINALE

I hadn't walked more than a half-dozen steps into the convenience store before the clerk noticed me. Of course, noticing customers was part of her job, but this time it was something special, watching her head turn around quickly, her eyes large with surprise.

To be perfectly honest, I would have been a little bit disappointed if she hadn't been startled. After all, how often, even in a university town the size of Norman, Oklahoma, do you see a guy dressed in medieval garb, hooded cape, fur-lined leather vest, and chain mail, come walking out of a cold January night?

Not that the girl, who looked to be about twenty and was wearing a blue smock with the store's name on it, had anything to say about looking unusual. The pink and green dyed hair and nose ring were probably not listed in the store's employee manual. If this little mom-and-pop place had one.

"Something I can help you with?" she asked.

"No thanks, "I said.

The store wasn't that big. I could find what I needed without a problem. I mean, how difficult is it to hide the chips and the French bread? I grabbed what I needed, along with a six-pack of Pepsi. There would probably be plenty of the things I liked to drink at the party, but I didn't want to take a chance.

As I turned to head towards the counter I heard the buzz that announced the front door opening. That sound could easily get very annoying, though I imagined that after a while you learned to screen it out. The new customer was a lean man, dressed in an overcoat, a scarf wrapped around his neck, and a pipe emitting smoke from cherry tobacco, held between tightly clenched teeth.

"Be anything else for you?" the girl asked when I set my stuff down. Before I could answer she began picking things up and running them in front of the barcode scanner attached to the cash register.

"So, aren't you a little late, or are you just really, really getting a jump on things?" she asked.

"No, I don't think I'm late," I said, with a quick glance at the big Coors clock behind the counter. My watch was in the belt pouch hanging around my waist and a bit hard to get to. It was only a quarter past nine. The party would just be getting started.

"Well, if you're dressed like that for Halloween, then I would say that you're about a couple of months late. If it's for that Medieval Fair, it's not supposed to roll around until April, and the last time I looked it was still January," she said.

"January sixth, to be precise," said the man with the pipe, putting a loaf of bread down in front of him and gathering up a newspaper from the nearby rack.

I waited until he was heading out the door, to the accompaniment of the same annoying buzzing that had announced his entrance, before I said, "Who was that masked man?"

"Was he really here at all? Or did we just imagine him?" the girl chimed in. "So, what's so special about January 6th?"

"It's called Twelfth Night. Have you ever heard that old song "The 12 Days of Christmas""?

"Yeah, my grandmother used to love to sing it at the holidays. All about turtledoves, peacocks, and a bunch of dorky lords a leaping and stuff like that, isn't it?"

"Sort of," I said. "In medieval times they actually stretched out the celebration of Christmas over 12 days, starting on December 25 and ending on January 6. That's where the name Twelfth Night came from. It was the night of the biggest celebration.

"I belong to a local medieval reenactment group. Every year we hold a big blowout party on or as close as we can get to the sixth of January. This year it's on a weekend so we actually get to celebrate it on the right day."

"Wild, man. So, do all the women come and run around like tavern wenches or damsels in distress?" asked the girl. She began putting my purchases into a big brown paper sack "That'll be eight fifty."

I laid a twenty-dollar bill on the counter. "As for the women in our group, they come as whatever they want, and party with the best of them. By the way, my name is Conner, Conner McManus. What's your name?"

She arched her head slightly as if giving me the once-over. "Nikita. Before you ask, no I'm not Russian. I just like the name, and yes, I picked it."

"Works for me," I said. In the medieval group we all picked out medieval-sounding names and went by them. "Think maybe you would like to go to the Twelfth Night party with me? I can come get you when you get off. It'll be going on all night."

"Don't bother coming back to get me," said Nikita, a note of finality in her voice.

I had expected her to say no. This girl didn't strike me as being too interested in things medieval. Hey, it wasn't the first time I had been turned down for a date and it certainly wouldn't be the last. "Well, maybe another time."

Nikita pulled her smock off and tossed it on the floor. She twisted the key in the lock of the register, then pulled it out and dropped it down a small slot in the back of the counter. Grabbing an army surplus field jacket from a peg on the wall, she slipped it on.

"Why come back later since I'm going with you now?"

"I didn't really like that place anyway," Nikita explained. "I'd been planning on quitting on Monday. It was boring. The guy who owns the place was such a grouch; besides, I think he wanted to fuck me."

Nikita spat on the floor as she talked about the storeowner, which didn't bother me a bit. I knew that guy, and her description pretty well summed things up. Besides, it was her floor, in her apartment, and she could do anything she wanted.

The Twelfth Night party was set in a converted church a few blocks from the convenience store. I knew from past experience that there was virtually no parking in front of the place, so I had left my van in a lot behind one of the administration buildings just a couple of blocks away.

Nikita had been insistent that we stop by her apartment so she could change clothes. Since it was only a block or so out of the way I didn't see any need in retrieving my van.

"It won't take that long. Not to mention that you said yourself the party was going to go on all night."

"Well, M'lady, far be it from me to deny you the chance to get all gussied up."

"Look, if you 're going to start sounding like Lord Billy-Bob Clampett I may just have to kick you where the chain mail don't shine."

"Actually," I mused, "the place you're talking about probably gets pretty shiny. You know, all that rubbing against a saddle and whatnot."

Nikita didn't say a word, just produced a key, and opened the door. Her apartment was the top half of a two-story house. From the mailboxes, it looked like the bottom floor had been cut up into two apartments.

Not that the three rooms - kitchen, living room, and bathroom - were all that big. A large mattress filled one end of the living room. The only other furniture was a table, some scrounged kitchen chairs, and a bookcase made from bricks and boards.

Nikita murmured something before she disappeared into the bathroom, which doubled as a closet since I could see some clothes hanging from the wall.

I walked over to her bookcase and scanned the titles. Most were fantasy, Tolkien, Howard, de Camp, and Drake, with a few horror titles thrown in, as well. I felt a sense of relief when it occurred to me that there wasn't a romance title in the bunch. Not that I had a problem with a girl who read romances, mind you.

Peeking out from a small niche between the bricks and the wall was another book.

It crossed my mind that this might be her diary. I considered for a moment just leaving it and respecting her privacy, but prurient curiosity won and I pulled the slim volume out where I could see it.

It was the size of a paperback book and was bound in worn leather. I flipped through a couple of pages. The paper felt like old, old parchment. There was neat precise writing inside, broken up every couple of pages by drawings done in such fine detail that it was scary to think they had come from a human hand.

I'm not sure when it occurred to me that it wasn't written in English, but rather in Latin. It had been a half dozen years since my last Latin class, the result of an attempt at a Catholic education by my parents, so I had forgotten most of it. But here and there I did recognize a few words. There was something about hounds, and it looked like the word hunt reoccurred a number of times.

"Curious and curiouser," I muttered.

"So, is there more to this Twelfth Night thing than just a last night of Christmas party?" asked Nikita.

I shoved the book back into its hiding place.

"Yes, as a matter of fact. There are some cultures that considered the time between Samhain, that's Halloween, and the end of Christmas to be a Season of Misrule, where everything got flipped on its head. The peasants could be kings and the rich act as servants. That sort of thing."

"Cool," she stepped out of the bathroom. Nikita had replaced her jeans and tee shirt with a long black sheath dress, a chain mail belt, and dagger riding on her hip.

"So, will I fit in with your medieval crowd?"

Okay, so the pink and green hair wasn't exactly what you would have seen on the dance floor in the halls of Richard the Lionhearted, but everything else worked for me. She walked up to the edge of the bed, just in front of me. "Well?" she asked.

I bowed, took her hand, and kissed the back of it.

"I ought to let you know that there are a few of the people I usually hang with who would say that gesture alone would suggest you were gay and would want to beat the crap out of you."

"That's their problem." Three years army special forces and ten years of martial arts training were enough to let me know I could handle most anything. "As for my sexual orientation, that's none of their business, either."

"We can discuss that part in more detail later." She touched the edge of the bed with her foot. "But right now, m'lord. I believe you promised to take me to a party."

"Indeed I did."

The roar of a motorcycle just below the apartment window seemed to shake the very foundations of the building. A moment later the sound was gone and replaced by the baying of a dog.

Nikita went stiff, the color draining out of her face, her grip on my arm tightening to the point of cutting off circulation.

"What's the matter?" I said.

"That, that, dog. I don't like dogs. I never have."

I went over to the window and looked around. There was nothing there, just a couple of trash cans, an empty packing crate, and signs left over from a garage sale the previous week. I wasn't sure just what I had been expecting, the vicious glowing specter of the Hound of the Baskervilles or what.

"It's okay," I said, gently. "If you want, we don't have to walk to the party. I can go get my van and come get you here."

"No, no. It…it was nothing," she said. "Just put it down to my being frightened by a Chihuahua with an attitude when I was a little girl."

"If you're sure."

"Trust me; the last place I want to be tonight is by myself."

Anyone who happened to drive past the old church that night, or any other night, for that matter, would have not paid much attention to it. All they would have seen would have been a red brick building, bracketed by heavy bushes, with a huge round stained-glass window above the door.

The place hadn't actually been a church for over ten years. Five years ago, friends of mine, Al and Kathy Jennings, had bought it and begun to convert it into their dream home. The results had been spectacular enough to merit an appearance on a national television series devoted to unusual homes.

As we walked in, I recognized most of the people who were already there and had a pretty good idea of who would come drifting in over the next few hours. Some were friends of long-standing, others people whom I knew by name but had barely even spoken to.

The place was not huge, but it felt like it. There was a single downstairs room with a kitchen in the back, while an upstairs balcony wrapped around the second floor, hiding the family's private quarters. Everywhere there hung banners carrying household and personal badges, flowers that wrapped around the stained-glass windows, and an assortment of weapons and musical instruments on the walls.

Nikita and I deposited the items I had bought on the buffet table near the kitchen door. There was food of all sorts, from what passed for traditional medieval dishes to things that had the distinct look of having come from local fast food places.

"Your friends here sure know how to lay out a spread," said Nikita.

"Oh, yes. There are some very, very good cooks here tonight. You will not go home hungry. But just be glad that one cook didn't bring anything."

"Just who would that be?"

"Me."

"And just why is that a good thing, then, that you didn't cook?" she asked.

"Less chance of fatalities," I laughed. "I'm honest enough to admit that I'm not a very good cook."

I filled up two pewter mugs with hot apple cider and passed one to Nikita. She sniffed it, and then took a hesitant swallow.

"Don't worry; I didn't spike it with anything. Although there is a whole selection of much stronger drinks available, should you desire one."

"Don't worry, m'lord, you don't have to get me drunk to have your way with me. If I choose to let you," Nikita said.

"I'll remember that."

Just then two men with lutes, a woman with a harp, and a couple of drummers who had set up in one corner of the room began to play.

It occurred to me that if two hours ago someone had told Nikita she would be listening to Celtic music, and hopefully enjoying it, she would have likely not believed it. After three songs I noticed her mouthing the words, almost in sync with the musicians.

Several couples had moved out into the center of the room, clearing away a couch and a couple of chairs, and begun to organize a group dance. I touched Nikita on the shoulder.

"Would you care to dance?"

"I'm not sure," she hesitated. "This is a bit far from a rave or a mosh pit. I think I can pick up the steps if I watch for a few minutes. Then, if you're still interested..."

"I stand ready for you, m'lady."

I heard my name called from the back of the room. Standing at the door to the kitchen was the owner of the house, Al Jennings, or, as he was known in the group, Jon de Vitte. I knew him for three years by that name and when I learned his real name, it just never seemed to fit him, at least in my mind.

"Jon! How come you let them keep conning you into hosting this little shindig year after year?"

"Hey, you know me, I'm an easy mark. Kathy just smiles sweetly and I give in, despite my best intentions. Look, can you give me a hand? I need some help to bring in a table from the garage. I'm seriously thinking that we are going to need it."

The garage was a separate building, about thirty feet from the main house, as solidly built out of heavy red brick as the church itself. The whole backyard was wrapped in the same sort of bushes that wound around the front. There were several leafless trees whose bare limbs hung like specters in the moonlight, marking the path to the garage.

Normally, the porch and backyard would have been full of people indulging in a tribute to the nicotine demon. This time there were just Jon and me, along with the cold and the full moon.

We had just swung the garage door closed when the sound of dogs howling filled the night, echoing off the building and the trees. It seemed to come from everywhere and nowhere at once. I had an eerie feeling of déjà vu, times a hundred.

The same way it had happened at Nikita's apartment, the sound was suddenly gone, leaving a loud silence in its wake. Jon and I just looked at each other, neither of us seeming to want to say anything.

Finally, a grin rolled across his face and Jon said, "So who let the dogs out?"

"Or who chased them back in?" I asked. "I think the technical term for that little bit was…just plain weird."

"I love it when you talk dirty," laughed Jon.

I was about to grab my end of the table when I looked back toward the alley gate. Someone stood there, a tall man, dressed in a leather jacket and black leather riding chaps.

I thought I caught a glimpse of a motorcycle behind him. I couldn't see his face; it was too dark.

I assumed it was just someone arriving late and coming in the back way. No doubt he had his change of clothing in saddlebags on the cycle. I couldn't have turned my head for more than a second, but when I looked back, he was gone.

The roaring of motorcycles filled the backyard for a few seconds and then faded in the distance.

"What was that term you used earlier? Just plain weird?" said Jon. "I don't know if that qualifies, but it's close."

"Yeah," I grabbed up my end of the table and we headed back inside.

Finding Nikita wasn't too hard. The house wasn't that big, no matter what it felt like. She had moved away from the area where the dancing was going on to talk to another woman whom it took me a second or two to recognize. This was an old friend, Lady Serina de Lyman, who in the real world answered to the name Serina Smith. She wore a long crimson Italian Renaissance dress that looked like it had been designed for her.

"Lady Serina? I might have known. It looks like I came back just in time. I suspect that you two ladies have been plotting and planning."

"Of course we have, Conner," laughed Serina. "And you are to be the victim of all our plans. I would suggest that you be on your best behavior. I've been telling Nikita all about you, every nasty little detail."

"Oh, boy, I'm in deep trouble." Actually, Serina could tell her a lot about me, things I would prefer didn't get around. Our families had been friends for years and we had known each other since sixth grade. "As I suspected, Lady Serina, you are being a very bad influence on this innocent newcomer to our gathering."

"M'lord," she said with a sly smile. "I do my best to be a bad influence, wherever I can. Now, if you will excuse me. I must go forth to spread chaos and terror in my path."

"It was nice meeting you, Serina," said Nikita. Turning to me she said, "Serina told me that I was a very lucky girl. That you are one of the nicest, most considerate men she has ever known."

"Well, Serina doesn't get around much," I laughed.

"No. I'm beginning to get the idea, Conner Ryan McMannus, and she told me that that is your real name, that you are a man of many facets. I wish I had the time to explore them all. I have a feeling that your walking into the store tonight was one of the better things to happen to me lately.

"We'll see." I leaned forward and put my hands on Nikita's shoulders, drawing her closer to me. I could feel a moment's resistance as if she were unsure. Then as lips met it was as if she were trying to push herself closer and closer to me, her arms wrapping tight around me. I've been kissed before, but nothing like that.

In the back of my mind a little voice was saying, "Man, hold onto this woman."

For a long time the only thing I could feel was the pressure of her lips against mine, and every inch of her body, breasts, legs, and hips pressing hard against mine, our hands digging into each other. I could imagine the sort of show that we were putting on for everyone around us. Frankly, right then I didn't give a rat's ass.

Naturally, that's when everything went wrong, very, very wrong.

The front door to the church blew open, slamming so hard against the wall that it nearly ripped itself free from the metal hinges that were anchored in the brick. There was no way a natural wind would do that. A couple that was standing close to the door barely got out of the way in time.

Two of the largest dogs that I had ever seen, like some mutated crossbreed of a wolfhound and an elephant, stood just inside the doorway. Other dogs surged around them into the church, growling as they went, herding the people back.

Out of the corner of my eye, I saw Jon come out of the kitchen, a very large battleaxe in his hand. Around the room, I didn't have to see to know that swords were being unsheathed and daggers drawn, weapons appearing in the hands of not only men but women, as well. I had a hunch that more than one person in the room was weighing their chances of reaching their cars where more lethal weapons might be found.

I still had my arm around Nikita. I could feel her muscles tightening with every passing second. "Just wait," I whispered, trying to give her a reassuring squeeze. "There may be a way out of here without anyone getting hurt."

"There isn't," her voice was husky and far away.

The dogs had cleared a corridor into the center of the room. From outside walked a man; dressed in the same black motorcycle leathers as the man I had seen standing at the garden gate. Another half dozen figures followed behind, clad in leather, their faces masked by scarves, goggles, and protective helmets. Behind them I caught a glimpse of a line of motorcycles, silently awaiting their riders' return.

The man came into the center of the room and turned toward Nikita and me. He raised his arm and pointed at her.

"No!" I said pushing her behind me. From all sides armed people took a step forward, ready to fight at my side.

"Conner!" I looked toward the balcony. Someone threw a sword to me. I have no memory of catching it or unsheathing the blade. I just knew that it was in my hand, ready to use.

"Now, I admit that was quite an entrance," I told the stranger. "But somehow I don't think that you and your friends are welcome at this party."

The stranger stood, unmoving. Then, with slow, precise movements, slipped off the helmet, holding it under his arm, and took off the scarf and goggles. His face was young, not more than thirty, but there was a haunted look in his piercing eyes.

"A brave man," he said. "Willing to fight, to defend this woman, even though he doesn't know what he might be fighting for."

"I suppose you're prepared to tell me."

The man's gaze shifted to Nikita. That same sad smile I had seen earlier was on her face now. "I am not the one who should do the telling."

"I think, I would prefer to hear it from you," I challenged. "Are you suggesting you have a claim on her?"

One of the dogs picked that moment to growl and charged me. I swung at it, intending to put my sword as deep into its body as I could. But the dog was just a bit too fast. Instead of connecting with the blade, I had to slam my hand, wrapped around the sword hilt, into the side of the dog's head to keep it from sinking its fangs into me. To say this was like hitting solid steel, and freezing cold steel, at that, would be a pretty good description of how much it hurt.

The dog yowled and was about to wrap his teeth around my arm when the man in front of me spoke a single word. The sound was soft and direct, literally pulling the animal back.

"You are brave," he said. "Through the years few have been willing to raise a blade to one of our hounds. Usually, they simply throw their arms up and hope to die quickly. Yet you fight."

"A man fights when he has to."

"Indeed. Perhaps you will understand more about us, and the woman, if you saw my brethren and myself in our traditional forms."

With that, he made a gesture with his hand and everything changed. Neither he nor his companions wore the motorcycle leathers that they had a moment before. Now all were dressed in various forms of medieval clothing, breeches, boots, and capes, their helmets adorned with stag horns, with swords and other weapons hanging at their sides. They pretty well seemed to fit in with the rest of us. Where there had been motorcycles now stood horses.

"Do you know me?" he asked.

"No, but that's one hell of a trick," I answered. "I'd say The Force is definitely with you."

"I am …."

"Prince Wilhelm Vladimir Dagget-Eletsky," said Nikita. "Once the ruler of a province in the Balkans. Now, cursed to ride forth as the Hunt Master for the Wild Hunt."

I had a bad feeling in the pit of my stomach, remembering that book I had found in her apartment. I looked over at Nikita, knowing that I would find her changed. Her black dress was gone, replaced by leather breeches, a tunic, a vest and a cape. All adorned with chain mail so fine that it was hard to tell the individual links. The green and pink hair were gone, replaced by a whitish-blonde braid that hung down her back.

"This night the Hunt rides forth for one reason alone," he intoned. "We have come to reclaim one of our own."

Nikita placed her hand on my cheek. "Conner, each of the Huntsmen is cursed to ride with the Hunt, instead of moving on to wherever souls go to find peace. I have been a part of this group for more than five hundred years.

"Do you remember how you said earlier that Twelfth Night was the last night of the season of misrule, where the peasants could be kings and everything was reversed? Also, during this season the barrier between the worlds is stretched thin and one of the Hunt can walk among humans again, to taste what it is we are cursed, to be reminded of all that we have lost."

"This year it was Nikita's turn," said the Hunt Master.

"No," I said. "Take me instead. Let her live out the time that would have been mine. I will ride at your side for however many eternities is the price to free her soul."

The Hunt Master chuckled. "That cannot be."

Tears rolled down Nikita's cheeks. "Conner, soon not even you will remember me. It will be as if I was never here. No one at the convenience store, even the grumpy owner, will recall I worked there. If you go to my apartment you will find a couple living there who know nothing of me. That is the price each of the Hunt pays for these few brief days where we walk as human again, the knowledge that no one will remember our time among them. I knew this was the last night of the season that I was free. I did not want to hurt you, but I did not want to recall what was going to happen."

I kissed her again, pulling her to me as tightly as before. When she finally stepped away I felt like part of my heart had been ripped out.

"If I recall the legends of the Hunt correctly, within limits your magic is strong," I said to the Hunt Master.

"Within limits."

"Then grant me a simple request. Let my memories of Nikita remain mine. Let her ride with you, but know that someone remembers her."

"You are a brave man," he said. He drew his sword, the hounds growling around him, and then touched it against my blade. Very gently he laid a gloved finger against my forehead. "It shall be as you wish. I hope in the years to come you will not regret your choice. Remember Nikita, remember us all, my friend."

I watched as the Hunt left our hall and mounted their horses. One had been brought for Nikita. Then they all disappeared into the night, the hounds running beside them.

I stood on the porch for a long time after they were gone, not sure what to do.

'There you are," said Serina, handing me a glass of wine. "Don't look so long-faced. This is a party. You're supposed to be having fun."

"I'm doing my best. I guess I'm not in a party mood right now."

"Maybe I can get you in a better mood, later. Come on back inside."

"Okay."

"Can I ask you something, Conner?"

"Sure."

"Did something weird happen tonight?"

"No weirder than normal, I would say," I laughed.

"That's a relief."

## The End

# ABOUT OUR CREATORS

## WRITER -

**BRADLEY H. SINOR** - has been writing for five/sixths of his life, and has written many short stories, most of them published in a variety of anthologies and three short story collections. His new collection – The Game's Afoot: A Sherlock Holmes Miscellany, published by Pro Se Productions – is now available on Amazon. He lives in Tulsa, OK, with his wife, (writer and copy-editor) Sue Sinor, and three cats. He can be contacted on his Facebook page as Brad Sinor.

## INTERIOR ILLUSTRATOR -

**WARREN MONTGOMERY** - has been in the comic book industry since 1988. He has produced comic book lettering for such publishers as Boneyard Press, London Night Studios, Bluewater Comics, Simon & Schuster, and BOOM! Studios, and has colored for many small press publishers. He currently self-publish under the Will Lill Comics banner. Born in Chicago, he currently lives in Portland, Oregon. (twm1962@yahoo.com) (www.wlcomics.com)

## COVER ARTIST -

**ROB DAVIS** - began his professional art career doing illustrations for role-playing games in the late 1980s. Not long after he began lettering and inking, then penciling comics for several small black and white comics publishers- most notably for Eternity Comics, which eventually became Malibu Comics in the 1990s, on their book SCIMIDAR with writer R.A. Jones. Branching out to other black and white publishers and eventually working at both DC and Marvel Rob worked on likeness-intensive comics like TV adaptations of QUANTUM LEAP and STAR TREK's many incarnations mostly on the DEEP SPACE NINE comics for Malibu. At Marvel, he worked on the Saturday morning cartoon adaptation of PIRATES OF DARK WATER. After the comics industry implosion in the late 1990's Rob picked up work on video games, advertising illustration, and T-shirt design as well as some small press comics like ROBYN OF SHERWOOD for Caliber. Rob continues to do the odd self-published comic book as well as publisher and designer for his small-press production REDBUD STUDIO COMICS. Rob is Art Director, Designer, and Illustrator for the New Pulp production outfit AIRSHIP 27 partnered with writer/editor Ron Fortier. Rob is the recipient of the PULP FACTORY AWARD for "Best Interior Illustrations" in 2010 for his work on SHERLOCK HOLMES: CONSULTING DETECTIVE and has been nominated for the same award every year since. He works and lives in central Missouri with his wife and two children.

# THE BATTLE OF THE IMMORTALS

Angus Drake and Jayne Montrose are immortal, members of a select group of humans endowed with this eerie gift. Throughout the ages they enjoy playing elaborate pranks on one another to alleviate the boredom of their existence. When Jayne is captured by an old rival named Erin De Costa, Drake and chum Warren set off to rescue her.

In 1596 the famous Spanish jeweler and silversmith, Don Jose Damon du Juan created a beautiful carnet for Jayne made of a multifaceted red ruby in a silver setting. Considered one of the finest pieces of art ever created, it was supposedly lost at sea many years later. Erin informs Jayne that "Eye of Dawn" is actually in a museum and wants Jayne to steal it for her. If she refuses, Erin will kill several children she has kidnapped from an orphanage Jayne opened decades earlier and continues to support.

With innocent lives in the balance, the battle of the immortals has begun.

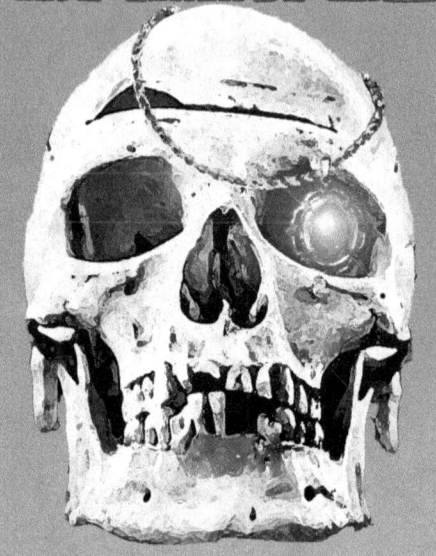

## Pulp Fiction for a New Generation!

Airship27Hangar.com

NEW PULP

THE EYE OF DAWN

Bradley H. Sinor

www.ingramcontent.com/pod-product-compliance
Lightning Source LLC
Chambersburg PA
CBHW051123260626
47170CB00005B/1632